Ant and Cleo Book 1

Ant and Cleo, Volume 1

Dominic Green

Published by Dominic Green, 2024.

Table of Contents

What reviewers have said about the *Ant and Cleo* series:

"...absolutely a hoot and the concept really allows for imaginations to run riot."

"All in all a very entertaining story, well written and edited. I would look for more from this author."

"Although this series is written for children, there's a lot for grown-ups that children wouldn't get..I thoroughly enjoyed episodes 1 to 5 and can't wait for the sixth."

"...a great story and is told well..good dialogue and characters and a story that has plot, surprises and pace."

"...a ripping yarn set (mostly) in space...I look forward to downloading more in the series."

"The author has a dry sense of humour which often had me chuckling out loud."

"The author borrows with humour from many American and British science fiction, espionage and fantasy genres, to create truly original, intelligent and funny stories with likable characters and a space opera setting. Each book can be read independently but it is best to read them in order. I highly recommend these books to those who don't take themselves too seriously and like works of imagination."

Praise for Dominic Green's *Smallworld:*

"...a showcase for Green's bone-dry satire and deadpan humour...Green's agile imagination constantly wrong-foots the reader. A delight."

Peter Ingham, *The Telegraph*

1 - Down In The Woods

"Course it's got vipers. Issa *forest*, innit? Bin ere since King Arold oo got shot in the eye by Robin Ood."

Ant's dad spat at a passing squirrel. Ant had hoped the squirrels here would be red, with pointy ears. Like every other squirrel in England, they were grey and tufty.

"I thought Old English forests were all deciduous", said Cleo.

Ant's dad turned round and stared at Cleo as if she'd been a large, red, pointy-eared talking squirrel.

"Deciduous? Wossat mean then?"

He grinned a huge row of horribly maintained teeth at Cleo, then carried on heaving stuff into the back of the truck.

"He does know what it means", whispered Ant to Cleo. "He taught me what it meant. It means the opposite to evergreen."

Cleo looked puzzled. "Why does he pretend he doesn't know, then?"

Ant shrugged. "I dunno. Sometimes he just seems to enjoy pretending to be a moron."

Ant's dad continued to load stuff into the truck. Ant suspected the truck should not be parked here. It was illegal to park anywhere that came straight off a motorway, wasn't it? This little service road wasn't the sort of road you normally left a motorway on, and it had had a sign saying SERVICE VEHICLES ONLY in big red-and-white letters.

It was amazing how loud the motorway was, even here in the trees. Ant's dad's eighteen-wheeler was parked well back in the pines, where a passing traffic cop would only see it if they craned their necks back and to the left while they sped by. Still, the truck / trailer combination was the length of a row of houses, a difficult thing to miss. Ant's dad was using the trailer's tail lift to load pallets that had been poorly stacked with gigantic drums of something. It was impossible to see inside the drums, but what was inside sloshed and slopped like a liquid.

"What's in the drums?" Ant had said to his dad as he grunted and struggled under one.

"Green diesel", his dad had said, and winked, and had not explained further.

The two men who had delivered the drums stood by watching him load them, not helping in any way. Their truck, parked a few yards further back in the trees, still had its engine running. The only other thing parked in the layby was an old Luton van, so badly rusted that its numberplate was held on with wire and its boot held shut with a padlock. The two drum deliverymen had investigated the Mysterious Van carefully when they first arrived, and seemed to have satisfied themselves that it presented no threat to them.

Eventually, Ant's dad heaved the last enormously heavy cylinder into the back of the York and began securing the tailgate. He had been manhandling drums since first light, and the trailer was kneeling heavy on its axles. The two men found their feet and approached him again.

"Well, it's been a pleasure doing business with fellow workers", he said. "This stuff'll keep our members going for a good month or more."

The bigger of the two men smiled widely at the smaller - a little more widely than Ant liked.

"There's just the question of payment", he said.

"Fellow workers", said Cleo to Ant quietly. "Your dad's a *communist.*"

"Of course." Ant's father fumbled in his back pocket for his wallet, too quickly. Ant noticed that his hands were actually shaking. There were not many men who made Ant's father shake, although the number of Saturday night fights he lost suggested he ought to be more afraid of other men than he was. The roll of cash he pulled out of his back pocket made both Cleo and Ant gape.

"I've not seen that many queens' heads on anything that folds before", said Cleo. "Magic! Your dad's a *criminal.*"

"If he's a communist, he's the richest communist I've ever seen", nodded Ant, who was thinking, *He doesn't usually have that much money. Where did he get that much money from without drinking it?*

"There's ten thousand litres here, right?" said Ant's dad, counting out odd-coloured notes that had *50* printed on them. Ant had never seen a fifty-pound note, and suspected his father had seen very few of them in his life too, but what else could they be?

One of the men shook his head. "Eight", he said. His accent made it sound like 'eeyat'.

"He's Irish", said Cleo, making a final decision. "Your dad's a *terrorist.*"

The money didn't change hands. But Ant's dad's voice was still shaky. "We agreed ten", he said.

The other man smiled. "Difficulties with supply. You know how it is."

"We agreed ten." Shaky though his voice was, Ant's dad was sticking to the guns embroidered in his tatty Arsenal cap.

"Let's get out of here", said Ant. "Based on past experience, this is about to get ugly."

***

The forest was green as diesel, and Ant suspected it would have been full of singing birds and the noises of squirrels scampering through undergrowth if it hadn't been for the constant roar of the motorway. But the local wildlife didn't seem to mind the sound. Usually, the sorts of places Ant's dad took him to were massive yards of tarmac supporting miles and miles of corrugated iron sheds, each one with a big company sign on the front saying things like ROTOWIDGET or BRITSTUFF PLC. Sometimes, the yards were on the Continent rather than in Britain, and the signs said GEMEINE DEUTSCHE DINGE GmBH or FRANCOTRUCS ET CIE, but the basic iron sheds were still the same.

"Sorry he had to bring you along", said Ant, chucking sticky darts at the back of Cleo's jacket.

"Thanks a lot", said Cleo.

"No, I didn't mean it like that. I mean, I'm sorry he let me bring you along when he knew he was going to be doing something tasty."

"Tasty?"

"Dodgy. Off the back of a lorry. Under the counter. Illegal. He's been hanging out with a worse and worse crowd since the start of the Fuel Protests."

"Cor." Cleo's face went wide. "Was all that illegal?"

"You knew bloody well it was!"

"No, I was only taking the mick. Your old man's a *Gangsta Rude Boy.*" Ant was not entirely sure what a Gangsta Rude Boy was, but it was said in a manner that suggested it was something to be greatly admired.

"What's a Gangsta Rude Boy?" said Ant.

Cleo shrugged, and kicked a pile of leaves. "I dunno."

"What are you doing tomorrow?"

Cleo grimaced. "My dad's taking me to work. It's the union's Take Your Kid To Work Day. He's going to wow me with all the really interesting stuff he does for a living."

"Think yourself lucky", said Ant, scoring a direct hit on the back of Cleo's hair extensions with a sticky dart. "For me, every weekday in the holidays is Take Your Kid To Work Day."

"Doesn't he think it's weird, you hanging out with girls?"

"I think he thinks you're my girlfriend."

"WHAT? That's GROSS!"

"I know, it's repugnant and disgusting. I have tried to dissuade him from this point of view, but he won't have anything different", said Ant. "He keeps winking at me and saying 'All right, squire, I know the score.' It drives me bloody mental."

Cleo grinned. Her grin seemed to go all the way round her head. "*I* think it's weird, you hanging out with girls. You're going to be playing with Barbie dolls and plastic vacuum cleaners next."

"*You* don't play with Barbie dolls and vacuum cleaners."

"I wouldn't play with Barbie dolls. There's a special Afro-Caribbean Barbie designed specially for black girls. Her name is Christie."

"No way."

"Yes way. But Christie isn't allowed anywhere near Ken, oh no. Christie comes with her own Afro-Caribbean boyfriend, whose name is Steven. Barbie and Christie are valuable educational aids that teach all us Afro-Caribbean girls what colour of boys we should be going out with. I could never go out with you, Ant, because you are Ken-coloured."

"I am so not Ken-coloured! Ken has one-piece plastic hair and a weird, smooth, underpant-shaped groin."

"Boys' dolls are better", said Cleo. "They have camouflage trousers and guns rather than hairdryers. And accessories that aren't pink. Do you know what happens to an Action Man head you put in the oven?"

"No, and I don't want to. Besides, Action Men aren't dolls. They're *Action Figures.* Hang on, what's this?"

Ant had no idea where the concrete strip had come from. There were similar strips all the way through the woods, suggesting that someone, at some time, had needed to drive heavy machinery into the trees. Maybe trucks for logging, he thought. His dad had said they still cut timber here, and that the woods were owned by the Forestry Commission. Ant's dad had made the woods seem really exciting, far more exciting than a weekend with his mum, at any rate. But the woods were not exciting. They were made of sharp-needled conifers with thin sappy trunks that were no use for climbing. In some parts, the trees were even planted in straight lines. Occasional bits of rubbish that a thousand picnickers had dropped were to be found in the undergrowth everywhere.

Certainly no-one was using the path for logging now. It was overgrown and cracked from side to side, with grass growing in the cracks.

"Maybe this used to be an airbase, and these were runways", said Cleo hopefully. "Before it was a forest, I mean."

"What, for *really small* aeroplanes?" said Ant. It was true. The concrete path would only barely have allowed a small van to squeeze through. Cleo giggled.

Then, she squinted into the trees, and pointed. "There's something parked up there."

Whatever it was, it was large, white, and definitely man-made.

Or at least, made by *somebody*.

The curves of it suggested a big heap of some stuff farmers liked to make big heaps of, covered with polythene, maybe weighted down with tyres for good measure. Farmers liked to make the landscape tidy by wrapping it in polythene, and they seemed to like making sure it didn't blow away by covering it in rubber too.

They walked further into the concrete clearing. The thing was not a thing made by any farmer. Nor would it have been any use in clearing or transporting logs.

It was roughly the shape of two woks, hubcaps, or indeed saucers, slapped together. On its front surface - or what Ant decided to think of as its front surface - a line of aerials and antennae poked out, with no clue as to their function. There were panels round the curve of its hull which might perhaps be opened to refuel or repair it, just like any other vehicle, for it was certainly a vehicle of some sort. There were also struts and rails attached to its underside to which ground crew might fix extra fuel tanks or other equipment that wouldn't fit inside it. On top of the thing, a bulge of hull was pinched up into a cockpit shape. It had a surface that might be glass or plastic, but which reflected light like a huge, teardrop-shaped mirror. Two small vanes, far too small to be aeroplane wings, protruded from what Ant decided to call its fuselage, though fuselages were seldom saucer-shaped in his experience. The whole thing was about the size of a large caravan - one of the big ones that old people sometimes drove down the road to live in at weekends rather than staying in their own houses.

"It's an aeroplane", said Cleo, with something less than total conviction.

This aeroplane, though, had neither ailerons nor engines, and the dull and faded lettering that swirled around its hull was not in any alphabet Ant recognised.

Most unsettling, however, was what the thing was resting on - or rather, wasn't. Its complete lack of wheels, skids, struts or bricks-propped-under-axles only became apparent when Ant and Cleo bent down and squinted underneath the thing and saw nothing but the forest on the other side of the clearing. The thing was certainly *some sort* of aeroplane, for it was hovering in mid air.

It was, by now, absolutely certain what was being dealt with here.

"It can't be", said Cleo.

"No", agreed Ant. "Not parked up in broad daylight like a Ford Fiesta."

Then the man who'd been in the clearing with them all the time, and who they'd both either not noticed or simply ignored because the thing in the clearing had been more interesting, cleared his throat, and said: "Hello there, boys."

He was wearing a sweater and coat - the sort of thing a man might wear if he stood outside in the cold for a living. He was also wearing a pair of binoculars. He didn't wear them, though, in the way that people normally wore binoculars, slinging them around their necks - these binoculars were a big, complicated-looking assembly of lenses strapped directly onto his forehead, under which he grinned at Cleo and Ant as if they saw men with binoculars strapped to their heads every day of their lives.

"What are you doing out here on your own?" he said, as if being out on their own on these woods was in some way illegal. Ant hoped it wasn't.

"Who's he?" said Cleo. "I thought you said this place was open to the public."

"There's only two sorts of people who wear jumpers, coats *and* ties", said Ant under his breath. "Racetrack tic tac men and policemen. Leg it."

They legged it.

Unfortunately, he legged it after them.

First of all, he gained on them, having the advantage of longer legs to leg it with, even though he was wearing shoes that were no good for the purpose. But once they dodged into the woods under the overhanging branches, their pursuer became curiously unwilling to carry on running headlong into facefuls of twigs and needles, and there were no more footsteps crashing through the brush behind them. Ant and Cleo cowered in a bush and squinted back through the trees to see their attacker talking into what looked like a big mobile phone, and was probably a two-way radio.

"Maybe he's talking to his bookie", said Cleo hopefully.

Ant shook his head. "Not a chance. He's a copper all right. Probably here to nick dad. We've got to get back and warn him."

The man's voice could be heard clearly - perhaps he was unaware of how close they were to him.

"*Got two unwanted guests. Afraid so. Only kids, one cauc, one afro. Ran off into the woods north before I could catch them. Over.*

"*Weren't wearing hiking boots, and didn't look tired on their feet. Came here on bikes, maybe? Still no cars in the parking area for the picnic site, Dave, over?*

"*There's no other places a car could park. We've secured the roads all the way round the forest. It has to be bikes. Maybe they hid them, over.*

"*Well look again. The kids are here. They're hiding in the bushes about thirty yards away. Probably think I can't see them, over.*"

Ant looked at Cleo.

"We get the blooming heckfire out of here *now*", said Cleo.

Ant nodded. "Maybe we can circle around back to the truck."

***

Minutes later, covered in muck, moss, grass seed and sticky darts, they were not much closer to the truck. Navigating towards the roar of the motorway, though, they were making headway.

"I think he wasn't a man at all", panted Cleo as she struggled over a log. "I think he was an *alien*."

"Looked like a man to me. Only real human beings look that ugly."

"That was a *flying saucer,* man! With all alien writing all over it."

Behind them, the voice of Binocular Man could still be heard. It was fainter, but that might have been the sound of traffic.

"*I can see you, boys! No use running away from me! It'll be dark soon, and I can see you even then, and what'll you do then when you can't take a step without running into a tree CRASH AAARGH.*"

"Maybe those binocular things let him see in the dark", said Cleo.

"They must be tough at any rate, he's bumped into four or five trees in them already", said Ant defiantly. "And they don't seem to be able to let him see you're a girl, either. And besides, *I* know a *short cut*."

"Where?" said Cleo - and then, after she had followed Ant down the next bank:

"Oh, yeah. *That.*"

***

Running down the motorway hard shoulder was faster than running through the underbrush, and Ant doubted the Binocular Man could see them through the banks of earth either side of the road, even if he *could* see in the dark. As cars whizzed past, Ant hoped that none of them contained plain clothes policemen.

"Most police cars are Vauxhall Omegas", he said to Cleo. "Watch for Vauxhall Omegas."

"What do they look like?"

"They've got three headrests in the back."

"That means we'll only be able to see them after they pass us, numbnuts."

"DOWN! This is the bridge!"

They crouched behind a roadside crash barrier to stare down at the layby where Ant's father was illegally parked. There were still three trucks at the roadside. There were also three other vehicles. One of them was a car, a gigantic glittering black thing of the sort Ant's dad's friends cut up and made hot rods out of. Two looked like vans, but not vans of the sort that were painted white and contained mobile plumbers. These were black, and square, and large, and Ant had an uncomfortable feeling they were bulletproof.

There were also many, many men - men in camouflage fatigues, and men in suits and ties and overcoats. Most of the men in camouflage gear were wearing binocular headgear, and all of them were carrying rifles. The rifles were not the sort normally used by the British Army. They were very large and bulky, with holes drilled in the sides of their barrels.

In the centre of a ring of these men, Ant's father and the two Irishmen were kneeling on the tarmac with their hands cuffed behind them. Ant's father was bleeding from the face.

"*Dad*!" hissed Ant.

"They're probably going to Execute them", said Cleo learnedly, "as Terrorists."

Ant looked hard at Cleo, then moved along the crash barrier closer to the line of soldiers.

"Policemen don't execute anyone", he said, crossing his fingers mentally.

"They're not policemen", said Cleo. They're *aliens.*"

Ant snorted in derision, but Cleo shook her head with an air of vastly greater knowledge of alien species. "They came out of a flying saucer, didn't they? And why are they wearing those face masks? Because underneath, *their eyes aren't human.*"

Ant shrank behind the concrete support, hoping this was not true.

Then, one of the men in suits and overcoats, his face clearly visible as he wasn't wearing the same odd strap-on goggles as the others, walked up to Ant's father, who appeared to be spitting out teeth, and said to him, like an adult to a baby:

"Now, tell us again and we can avoid all this unpleasantness. Where is the Highwayman?"

"*- don't KNOW! Don't KNOW where the bloody Highwayman is! Don't even know WHO he is! Look in the back of my truck - only bloody GREEN DIESEL, for god's sake OOF.*"

Ant's dad was momentarily quiet as someone clubbed him in the kidneys with a rifle.

"*That* one's not an alien", said Ant. "He's got a human face."

It wasn't a pleasant face. It had probably been quite good-looking once, but a lifetime of scowling had made it sag like melted wax. It was human, though. The man's hair was corpse-grey, and his clothes immaculate, as if he checked himself over in every mirror he passed.

"He's probably been taken over", said Cleo, "by some Alien Mind Control Device."

One of the men in suits held up a device looking very like a TV remote control. A green light was flashing on it. Cleo pointed to the device and looked at Ant with an expression of immense superiority as if to say, *told you so.*

But then the man holding the device said: "He's telling the truth, I'm afraid, Alastair."

"You put too much faith in those things", said Alastair.

The other man smirked. "Care to tell it whether you've ever stolen government property, gone AWOL, or doodled a moustache on the picture of the Queen?"

Alastair didn't answer, but turned to face the ring of troops. "SPREAD OUT. LEAVE NO STONE UNTURNED AND NO BUSH UNBAYONETED. OUR MAN WON'T GO FAR WITH WHAT HE'S CARRYING. IF THE SIZE OF THE VAN HE USED IS ANYTHING TO GO BY, THE CONTRABAND MUST WEIGH HALF A TON."

Ant noticed suddenly that the back of the Mysterious Van was open. The doors appeared to have been cut open - probably by the acetylene torch he could see resting up against the side of the vehicle.

The soldiers left the layby and disappeared into the forest. Alastair raised a two-way radio and spoke into it.

"Simon, we've found his delivery vehicle in a motorway layby on the other side of the forest. What idiot was it who failed to realise the M1 runs through these woods? Have you found those children yet?"

Cleo and Ant gingerly edged back along the crash barrier and then, once the motorway embankment hid them from view from below, ran like flaming hell.

"NOW", they heard Alastair's voice crowing as they ran, "LET ME SEE. TERRORISTS FUNDING THEIR ACTIVITIES VIA ILLEGAL FUEL SMUGGLING. WHAT ARE WE GOING TO DO WITH *YOU?*"

***

"We're back at their Space Ship."

Ant shrugged. "They'll never suspect we'd go back here."

"Because it's bloody *mad*, that's why! Only a bloody *lunatic* would go back here! That makes us a couple of bloody *lunatics!*"

"I'm *interested.*"

"But they might take us back to their home planet or something."

"I'd be safe. You're a girl, though. They might stick probes up your bottom or implant an alien embryo in you or something. *Hold it."*

They stopped on the edge of the clearing. Someone else was already here.

***

The new man looked tired and thin, and had a haircut that suggested he spent a lot of his time in prison. He was wearing neither a suit nor combat fatigues, but a pair of Levi's which still had the label dangling from the back of them, and a maroon T shirt. The T shirt had aliens in flying saucers on it, along with the words SPACE RASTA. The aliens had enormous dreadlocks and were smoking intergalactic cigarettes of some description. The man was, however, clearly neither a Rasta nor an alien, being white-skinned and blue-eyed. He was also wearing new Nike trainers, and was trying to pull a load ten times his size in the direction of the Space Ship.

The load consisted of a variety of odd objects. There were plants that had tags from garden centres, and still others that appeared to have simply been dug out of the ground and wrapped in plastic. There was a pallet of fluorescent yellow spheres stencilled CAUTION FRAGILE DANGER OF DEATH, on top of which other objects seemed to have been dumped and slung with gay abandon. There were T shirts piled up saying GALLERIE DEGLI UFFIZI FIRENZE, MY FRIEND WENT TO SYDNEY OPERA HOUSE AND ALL I GOT WAS THIS LOUSY T SHIRT, and I'VE BEEN TO DISNEYLAND. There were homespun shawls covered in pictures of what looked like llamas in orange, white and black thread. There was an immense wooden table so thickly covered in carvings that it befuddled the mind. There was a snowstorm globe the size of a human head, with a cathedral the size of a baby's head in the centre of it, and a nameplate saying IL VATICANO.

There was food and drink, too - for some reason, mostly crisp packets in a bewildering variety of flavours and colours, on top of black puddings, boxes of tea, jars of jam, jars of Marmite, and many, many bottles of different types of beer, gin and whisky. All the food and drink had probably been purchased at Tesco's. Ant suspected this because it was all still jammed inside a supermarket trolley, the chain of which appeared to have been sawed through.

On top of the plants, yellow spheres, shawls, T shirts, and other paraphernalia were various items of electronic, scientific and heavy engineering equipment, all piled into a confusing jumble. Ant recognised a mass spectrometer (although more, to be fair, by the words 'MASS SPECTROMETER' written on the outside of its plastic packaging than by any great familiarity he had with mass spectrometers). There was a conical-hatted plastic doll in a box which read A PRESENT FROM WALES. There was a conical-bodied, beaked thing which Ant recognised with dread as a Furby.

This whole unlikely jumble was resting on a platform about the size of an average warehouse pallet, made of the same weird material as the Space Ship. And like the Space Ship, it was resting on absolutely nothing. The man was pulling the platform on a long rope looped round handles on the platform edge. The platform edge had lights which were flashing urgently in red.

The man had seemed harmless up to this point, as he was so obviously exhausted, and particularly since he was towing the platform using one hand. The other hand flopped uselessly at his side, as if he had no feeling in it. It was bleeding.

"He's *hurt*", said Cleo.

But the man did not seem quite so harmless when he turned to see the two of them, let go of his tow rope, and proved to have been holding a gun in the hand he'd been pulling with. The gun was pistol-sized, but otherwise looked similar to the guns the Binocular Men had been carrying. It was very large, and was pointing directly at them.

Ant and Cleo put their hands up slowly.

The man threw Ant the towrope. It wrapped round his hand like a lasso.

Ant and Cleo put their hands down. The man nodded at the towrope. Ant took hold of it. The man crossed the clearing to his Space Ship, flipped open a panel in its seamless hull, and put his bloody hand into the cavity he'd opened. The whole side of the vehicle dropped open and became a ramp which swung down to the ground. Lights came on in the inside of the ship. Ant could see seats, consoles, dials, and rows of switches.

The man gestured with his gun in the direction of the ship.

"There's no need to be so rude", said Cleo.

"Maybe he can't speak English", said Ant. "Being from Alpha Centauri and all."

"Not from Alpha Centauri", said the man. "From Alpha Centauri! Ridiculous! From Lalande 21185, me."

He slumped against the wall of the ship, as if he needed it to hold him up. His eyes did not appear to be focussing on anything.

Ant and Cleo took hold of the rope and leaned on it, expecting the load to be almost impossible to move. It was actually easier than they'd thought, as it didn't have to be dragged across the ground or tugged along on wheels - but once it started moving, it was difficult to stop it. It crashed into the side of the ship with a clang. The man looked up and stared at them severely.

"Sorry", said Cleo.

With difficulty, and with the man waving encouragingly at them with the pistol, they managed to drag the platform into the hole in the hull, and then up into the inside of the Flying Saucer. Inside, things were surprisingly cramped for a vehicle designed by an advanced spacefaring species. The hydraulics assembly that raised and lowered the saucer's tail lift - Ant could only think of it as a tail lift, though the thing was clearly not an articulated lorry of any kind - took up much of the room. The space at the top of the loading ramp was cramped, not much larger than the floating platform the man was manhandling into it, and stray crisp packets scrunched against the walls as the platform screeched into place. It appeared to have been designed to fit into the ship, and clicked flush into clamps on the deck which the man then locked, with difficulty, with his gun hand. At the front of the cramped cargo compartment was a ladder leading upwards into a dimly-lit space where the backs of three chairs were visible in front of banks of switches, knobs and dials. Past the chairs and the knobs and dials, Ant could see trees, dim and distorted; he had been right to think the dome on top of the saucer was made of some kind of mirrored glass. He also noted with approval that the upholstery on the chairs was made of real leather. Alien or not, the man travelled in style.

After covering the locked-down floating platform with a sort of thick clingfilm rolled out of a slot in its side, the man jabbed at a control on the wall, and the ramp began to fold up into the Flying Saucer behind them. By now, they could hear shouts, and footsteps crashing in their direction through the undergrowth.

"It's the Binocular Men", said Cleo forlornly, staring at the loading door as it closed over what might be their last sight of Earth. "They were the good guys."

2 - One Small Step For A Man

The man settled into the seat, and tried to put his hands on the controls. One of his hands fitted into the grips on the throttle in front of the largest seat. The other hand tried ineffectually to swat at the lines of switches. The man seemed to have no control over it whatsoever.

He turned in his seat with a look of despair on his face, and used his bad hand to point vaguely in the direction of Ant.

"You", he said. "Be my right hand." He pointed at a bank of switches. "Trip the third switch from the left."

The shouts and crashings were now all around the machine, along with a crackling that sounded like many, many rifles being cocked. With some fear, Ant reached out to push the switch down. He got the wrong switch. Something inside the structure of the spaceship screamed like a scalded cat.

A voice that sounded as if it was talking through a megaphone came from outside the ship. Ant could not make out all of what it said.

"- TURN OFF YOUR PRIMARY DRIVE AND LEAVE THE MACHINE -"

"DON' YOU KNOW RIGHT FROM LEFT?" roared the man. "Turn it OFF!"

Ant turned it off, and pushed the right switch. The scalded cat noise subsided, to be replaced by a gentle purr. A line of green lights streamed across the console. Curiously, the lights were all labelled in English, although they were incomprehensible. They said things like COIL, COOL, ING, XER, and STD.

"Do what I say, 'zactly when I say it", murmured the man. "Or we all die. Pull that long lever back half way. NO, THE ONE NEXT TO IT."

Chastened, Ant Pulled The One Next To It. The man watched lights stream around the rows of consoles round the cabin, and flicked switches absently with his left hand, without seeming to need to look at them. Then he moved his hand back to the steering column.

"Now trip the big orange switch above my head."

Ant reached up and flicked the switch.

"THIS IS YOUR LAST WARNING", came the voice from outside. "OPEN THE HATCH AND SURRENDER YOUR VEHICLE OR WE WILL OPEN FIRE."

Then the vehicle took off like a bullet from a gun.

***

Ant and Cleo fell immediately as if the floor itself had swatted them like a giant cricket bat. Then the floor tilted as the nose of the ship thrust upwards, and they were squashed into the rear wall of the cabin. Ant gasped for breath, splayed out against the wall behind him, which was vibrating like the skin of a drum.

"Can't *breathe* - " gasped Cleo.

Gradually, Ant forced himself out of a state of panic, and told his lungs to heave themselves open and shut against the terrible pressure of acceleration. Outside, the air itself could be seen rushing round the cockpit, flowing in waves like water. The horizon surrounded them, and it was visibly bending like a longbow bent by a giant. Then, it tilted and rolled to port, and the ship was flying across it rather than up out of it once again. The pressure on Ant's lungs released, and he was able to claw his way across the floor back to the man's chair again.

A large green disc had lit up on the control console, and the man had slumped himself across it to watch it. He was bleeding onto the display, and had to wipe his own blood off the glass absent-mindedly with his cuff. The display looked like a radar screen, but as Ant moved his head to look at it, the red white and blue dots in the display moved too, as if there were actually tiny points of light scooting around inside a tank in the machine.

"What does it show?" said Ant, trying to make conversation.

"Three-dimensional radar display. White dot in the middle is Us. Red dots closing are Them."

"Who's Them?" said Ant.

"Tornados. Interceptors scrambled from Mildenhall. First line of defence."

"Tornado *fighters*? They're trying to shoot us down?"

The man nodded as if his head was very heavy. "Will if they can. Don't worry about them. Outrun them easily."

"What are the blue dots?"

"Aurora. Second line of defence. More difficult to outrun."

"What's Aurora?"

"If they get close enough for you to see, it'll be the last thing you *do* see." His good hand still on the throttle, he waved in the direction of a panel on the console with his bad hand. "Open that. Red lever inside. Pull it down when I say and ONLY when I say."

The big red dots had now spat out smaller red dots which were converging on the centre of the display. "What are those?" said Ant.

"Missiles from the Tornados. Outrun those easily."

"These Aurora things are faster than a *missile*?"

"Faster than turbodriven lightning." The man eyed the blue dots professionally. "Get ready to pull the lever - NOW."

Ant yanked the lever. The sky around them lit up with space ships, travelling round their own in convoy, reflecting the sun so brightly that Ant thought at first that their own ship had exploded. The outside surfaces of the ships glowed an eerie green, as if they were some weird type of firework.

"Is that what our own ship looks like from the outside?" said Ant.

"Exactly", said the man, and pointed at the cockpit of the nearest ship. Ant looked and saw his own face looking back at him.

"Only an image", explained the man. "Trying to fool the enemy into shooting the wrong us." The explanation seemed to take a lot out of him, and he stared bleary-eyed at a button on the control panel, as if expecting it to tell him whether to push it or not.

"Gosh", said Ant, looking at his image. "Am I really that ugly?"

The man nodded gravely.

"Cushty!" said Cleo. "Reinforcements!"

"No", said Ant. "It's only an illusion." He pointed out Cleo's face next to his own. Meanwhile, the man was flicking switches, turning knobs and examining dials like a sleepwalker, automatically, without appearing to think a great deal about what he was doing.

Then, finally, he swayed backwards, pointed at the console, and said:

"Push the blue button."

- and toppled backwards into his chair.

Outside the cockpit, the blue had gone out of the sky. Ant remembered from lessons at school that the blue in the sky was the result of sunlight being scattered in the air. The sky outside was black. That meant there was no longer any air.

They were on the edge of space. The blue dots on the display were closing.

There was only one blue button. It was marked *C+*. Ant pushed it. The universe changed.

***

The sky glowed, so hard it hurt the eyes. The cockpit blister of the ship seemed to darken like light-sensitive sunglasses, until the view was bearable. The ship was scudding through great billowing clouds of something Ant was certain wasn't air. In fact, the clouds looked oddly solid, as if the ship wouldn't just zip through one if it hit it.

"Where are we?" said Cleo.

"I don't know", said Ant. "In space?"

"Space is black", said Cleo.

"Then we're not in space", said Ant; and then, he muttered:

"Maybe not in time, either."

The wrenching acceleration of the trip out of the Earth's atmosphere had gone, but Ant felt cheated. He should by rights be feeling light as a feather and floating round the cabin. Instead, he was standing behind the pilot's chair, while the pilot dozed fitfully in front of him.

"He's asleep", said Cleo.

Ant examined the pilot carefully. He shook his head. He put his hand inside the sleeping man's jacket, and brought it out for Cleo to see, covered in blood.

"I don't think he's asleep", he said. "I think he's unconscious. He wasn't just wounded in the hand."

"Well, that's just fine", said Cleo angrily. "Just great. Now we're stranded in the middle of *wherever we are* without anyone who can fly this bag of bolts." She strode round the cockpit swatting at things. "Just look at the state of this place. You call this a flying saucer?" She picked up a half-eaten apple core by the stalk, then dropped it disgustedly into a corner.

It was true. The spaceship's owner did not appear to spend a great deal of time cleaning up. The copilot's seat was a mess of pork scratchings packets and beer bottles.

"Just look at this dial", she tutted, pointing at a dial on the console. "It's not even digital." She squinted at the maker's nameplate on the control console. "Just as I thought. Made in Britain. If this was a *Japanese* spaceship, it'd have cupholders and curry hooks -"

Ant gaped. "Made in *Britain?*"

"Hawker Siddeley Aviation, it says here."

"Cleo, there is something very wrong with a Flying Saucer that is Made in Britain."

Cleo seemed unconcerned. "Don't I know it. This passenger seat doesn't even adjust."

"And Hawker Siddeley Aviation stopped making planes years ago. The last thing they made was the Harrier jump jet. Only the Americans, Russians and Chinese have ever built man-carrying space ships, and none of them have ever built anything like this."

Suddenly, a chunk of space rock big enough to have baby mountain ranges of its very own tumbled past the window. Ant jumped. Cleo screamed. Ant pressed his face up against the window, following the thing with his eyes as it hurtled away. It hurtled so quickly that it was almost gone already. Parts of the rock were glowing, as if it was a piece of sinter that had just flown out of a furnace. Further in the distance, now that he was looking for them, Ant could make out other flying islands glowing in the dark.

"The clouds", he announced, "are not clouds. Every little particle in one of those clouds is an chunk just like that one."

"But where did it come from? If it'd hit us at that speed -"

"I don't know. And yes, we'd be toast. *Thin sliced* toast. Cut into *soldiers*." Ant shook the pilot gently. "Wake up." He turned to Cleo. "He won't wake up."

"If you shake him and he's injured, it could make it worse."

"He might bleed to death. And then we'll *never* get home."

"Is there a first aid kit around here anywhere?"

Ant hadn't thought of that. He searched round the walls until he found a small aluminium box bolted to the steel skeleton of the ship. It was painted white, with a red cross.

"What if a red cross is, like, alien for Self Destruct?" said Cleo.

Ant squinted at the alien box. Its underside said that it had been Made In England. He took it off the wall, and opened it. It contained bandages, plasters, a large bottle labelled 'Ethyl Alcohol', a huge number of tiny glass cylinders labelled 'Morphine Sulphate', and a box labelled 'Space Sickness Tablets - Do Not Consume Under Thrust'. There was also a syringe large enough to harpoon a small whale.

"I don't think there's much in here that'll do him any good", said Ant.

"The alcohol might do him some good", said Cleo. "If we pour it over him and set light to it, it'll cauterise his wounds."

Ant looked at her severely.

"What? I saw it in a movie, all right?"

They eased the man off the pilot's seat and onto the floor. He moaned, but didn't wake up. As he came free of the pilot's chair, it crackled as the dried blood parted from the seat. Blood was still coming out of him, but Ant noted that the rate of bleeding seemed to be slowing.

"He's a poor sort of alien", said Cleo. "Why couldn't we get abducted by an alien who didn't bleed so much, and stayed conscious?"

"We're going to have to take his clothes off to get at the wounds."

Cleo crossed her arms defiantly. "I ain't taking his clothes off. He can die for all I care."

"Easy. He isn't wounded anywhere you wouldn't see down a swimming bath. Help me get his shirt off."

They stripped him of his jacket and shirt, and found an ugly-looking wound in his side. Not really knowing what to do with it, they dabbed it with alcohol soaked into a bandage, but not too much, because this made him start moaning again.

"He's going to die, isn't he", said Cleo. Ant didn't know what to say in reply.

They wrapped a bandage round the wound, and tied it up with a safety pin Cleo had been using to tie a scarf round her waist.

"Whatever we do, anyway, we won't starve", said Ant, looking at the mountain of crisp packets spilling off the cargo platform.

3 - One Mountain of Crisp Packets Later

"I'm sick of Worcester Sauce flavour. Have you got any Prawn Cocktail?"

Cleo shook her head slowly. Ant could swear she had gained several stones. "It's all Mango Chutney flavour over here." She sat up and squinted at the cargo platform, bleary-eyed. "Are you *sure* we didn't find anything to drink in there but beer?"

Ant nodded sadly, and stared at the label on his beer bottle. "Iss strange - the more I drink of it, the more thirsty I seem to get." He hiccupped.

"I have *got* to get out of here by tonight", said Cleo. "I am going to a *party* tonight."

"I've heard of parties", said Ant. "What are they like?"

"You *mus'* get invited to *parties*" said Cleo, burping.

"Not really", said Ant. "I think most of the kids at school think being poor is catching."

"My dad likes me going round with you. He thinks it means he's still in touch with the proletariat."

"Whassa proletariat?"

"What lots and lots of poor people are called when they get together", said Cleo.

"What, like a Council Estate?"

"Sort of."

"Hey - the room is spinning round", said Ant. "We must be landing."

"Is *not* spinning round", said Cleo defiantly. "*You're* not spinning round."

"Ah", said Ant, holding up a finger. "But if the entire room is spinning round, we will both appear to be stationary from the standpoint of each other."

"Don' you hold your finger up at me."

Cleo rested her head back against the spaceship hull. "I do not know", she said, "what adults see in this stuff."

"My dad", said Ant, "sees things that chase him out of the window."

"How is our patient?"

Ant had forgotten their patient. He looked sideways to check on the patient, who was still breathing, though he had now turned a beautiful shade of pink. He also seemed to be doing rather a *lot* of breathing, perhaps rather more than he really should.

"The patient", announced Ant, "is fine."

Suddenly, the entire room shifted, as if the ship really *was* landing. The cargo pallet, fixed to the floor and secured with straps and sheets of polythene, did not move. The crisp packets, and all the crisp crumbs associated with them, floated gracefully into the air, accompanied by all the beer bottles. The patient rose into the air. Cleo rose into the air. Ant rose into the air, as if floating on a cushion of nothing. Ant's arms rose into the air. Ant's legs rose into the air. And Ant's stomach, the stomach he had just filled with beer and crisps until he could stand the thought of Smoky Bacon Flavour no more, rose with them.

"Oh, no", said Ant. "Not zero gravity *now*."

***

"YEEEEUCH!!!!"

The floor was covered with crisp crumbs, and with bits of crisp that had been all the way to Ant's stomach and back. The seats were covered in the stuff, the console and Ant himself were covered in it, and crucially, Cleo was also covered in it.

"For PETE'S SAKE, Ant, can't you control yourself for just one lousy minute??? This is DISGUSTING!!!

Ant did not care. His stomach hurt badly enough for nothing else in the universe to matter. Zero gravity had always seemed like fun for astronauts, but he could now tell anyone who would listen that it felt very little like being either Peter Pan or Superman. Did NASA astronauts feel like this?

Everything in the ship had been weightless for just thirty seconds, and then the weight had come back again. Unfortunately, those thirty seconds had been all Ant's vomit reflex had needed. It now had to be at least an hour since the gravity had suddenly turned itself back on; Cleo's complaining muscles, however, had not begun to tire yet.

Cleo lurched across the cabin. "I've GOT to clean myself up - oh, this is VILE - OMIGOD."

Ant forced himself to look. Cleo was staring at a panel she had opened in the wall.

"This toilet", said Cleo with a contempt she normally reserved only for disc jockeys and the criminally insane, "is for Men Only."

She held up a length of flexible hose, the correct use of which could only be imagined.

Ant sniggered.

"Maybe they don't have women on their planet", he said.

"Omigod. How am I going to fit myself into this. DON'T WATCH."

Ant took down a space helmet from the pressure suit on the wall, put it down over his head, closed the silvered visor and folded his arms solemnly.

"I can't do this. I can't do this. I will simply have to cross my legs till Planet Bong, or wherever it is we're going."

"Planet Bong", said Ant with an air of superior knowledge, "is not a planet, but a shop on Camden High Street."

"Ohhhhh ANT, we're going to spend FOREVER out here -"

"Or at least till the air supply runs out", muttered Ant to himself.

"We'll never see our mums and dads AGAIN -"

"Suits me", muttered Ant to himself. Two nights ago, his own dad had raided Ant's piggy bank for the third time that month, and then recycled part of the piggy bank money as Ant's pocket money the following day. Ant had marked the notes, and he'd had to mow the lawn to get them back.

Then Cleo said a thing which made him sit up sharp in his helmet.

"Ant - *the universe is back.*"

***

He raised his helmet visor. Small untethered objects were floating around the inside of the ship again. *Ant* was floating around the inside of the ship again. Luckily, his stomach had done all the throwing and spewing it needed to. Also luckily, most of the liquid yawn from last time seemed to have dried hard on the spaceship walls.

It was back, but it was not the same old universe. There was no Sun, no Moon, and no Planet Earth. Instead, there were three huge impostor Moons, each a different colour, each many times the size of the old Moon he remembered. There was a red Moon, a scarlet Moon, and a crimson one.

"That one's the Moon", said Cleo. "No - that one. No - that one. Erm."

"None of them are the Moon", said Ant. "There's no trouser-shaped piece on the right hand side where Neil Armstrong landed in the right leg. And there's no Oceanus Procul Harum, which is the big dark blot on the left that doesn't look like anything but another Oceanus Procul Harum. And it's *red*", he added.

"Maybe we're looking at the Dark Side", said Cleo. Ant went quiet. He hadn't thought of that.

There was no proper Sun either; instead, there was a dull red smouldering mass that seemed to fill up half the sky. The windows took a good half minute to adjust to it, and Ant was certain he'd get sunburn even through his silvered visor. With his visor down, he found he could look almost directly at it. It was circular, like the sun.

But the most peculiar thing of all was the planet.

It was certainly a planet; it was even a planet like Earth, with seas and continents and icecaps and the occasional swirling hurricane. But it wasn't Earth. The continents were Earth-coloured in their middles, a sort of brick red; but the oceans were a darker red, the colour of dried blood; and where the continents met the oceans, they were sometimes a dingy maroon colour, sometimes a vibrant auburn. The icecaps were pink. The clouds were scarlet.

"That's not Earth, is it?" said Cleo.

Ant shook his head.

"That bit there looks a bit like Africa."

"It's also covered in snow."

"It snows on top of Mount Kilimanjaro. Mount Kilimanjaro's in Africa."

"Granted. But there are parts of Africa that are not on top of Mount Kilimanjaro. Otherwise Mount Kilimanjaro would not be in Africa. It would be the other way round."

Cleo nodded grudgingly, but Ant suspected she did not really believe him.

They stared at their new universe for a long time.

Then, Cleo screamed.

"I'm *floating!"* she yelled.

"Have you only just noticed?"

She took a second more to think about it, and then announced: "I feel sick."

Ant sighed, yawned, and settled back in mid-air with his hands clasped ostentatiously behind his head. "Take a Space Sickness pill."

Cleo examined the Space Sickness pills minutely. "It says they're Not To Be Taken Under Thrust", she wailed.

"Well, don't Take Them Under Thrust, then."

"How do I know whether I'm Under Thrust or not?"

"Do you *feel* Under Thrust?"

Cleo thought a moment. "I suppose I'd know, if I was", she said. "Wouldn't I."

So saying, she swallowed half the packet. Ant was beginning to realise uncomfortably that he, too, was soon going to need the toilet.

"What's that thing over there?" said Cleo.

"What thing?"

"That bright thing. That saucer shaped thing that's, erm, coming our way, very fast."

***

It was a saucer like their own. But it was much larger, maybe the size of a Portakabin rather than a caravan. It was difficult to judge sizes in space, but the pilot's cockpit, if it *was* a pilot's cockpit, was much smaller in relation to the rest of the ship, being a rather tiny blister infecting the top of the main saucer shape rather than a dominant feature of the design. The leading edge of the ship bristled with aerials and needles and radar dishes, just like Ant and Cleo's own vessel.

"What are all those big holes along its bow?" said Cleo.

"No idea", shrugged Ant. "Probably intakes for jet engines."

"Air intakes", said Cleo witheringly, "in space."

"Maybe they only use their jet engines in an atmosphere", said Ant curtly.

"They're gun ports, aren't they", said Cleo.

"They're far too *big* to be gun ports", Ant said, hoping that this was true. "Besides, anyone advanced enough to travel in space wouldn't be using guns that fired bullets."

"Or jet engines", added Cleo.

The saucer also seemed, to Ant's inexperienced eye, to be in considerably worse condition. There were streaks of corrosion all over it, and places where the stuff of its hull seemed to have been replaced with patches of what looked worryingly like bacofoil. It was possible to see the joints between the plates its outer skin was made of.

"Crikey", said Cleo, "it's in even worse shape than *ours.*"

"It has a pilot", said Ant. "Ours doesn't."

Cleo floundered around in the air until she could flick herself in the direction of the control panel. "Does this thing have a radio? We could call for help - whoops, what did I turn on?"

The lights went off all over the ship.

"Erm", said Cleo. "Which button did I push?"

The alien saucer turned side-on to the light, and Ant saw a faded emblem stencilled across its side. A star in a circle, two rows of stripes like wings, and the letters USASN.

"We're saved!" he said. "It's friendly!"

"How do you know it's friendly?"

"It must be friendly! It's American!"

4 - Our Friends The Americans

Things went dark as the much bigger saucer of the other ship closed over the sun. Then there was a CLANG as the two vessels' hulls collided.

Then, suddenly, the wheel in the hatch door above their heads (which had originally been in the floor) began to rotate, as if someone or something else was turning it from the other side.

"What if it's not an American", said Cleo, shrinking back behind a chair in fear. "What if it's an Alien."

"Not much difference between the two in my experience", said Ant.

The hatch swung inwards on metal hinges that shrieked like a scalded cat being dragged down a blackboard. The cargo pallet pinged free of its fastenings - it had been clipped into place over the hatch - and floated free into the centre of the cabin, big, heavy, and covered in sharp corners. The metal of the hatch door was thick as a finger, and it banged hard against the saucer's hull as it flew back.

A voice said: "Sensor says the atmosphere's breathable. Normal oxygen nitrogen." Then, it became puzzled and said: "Traces of alcohol and hydrochloric acid."

The voice was American. Ant was reassured.

"Better watch your six in there, Billy Hank. Them alien sons of mothers might just breathe alcohol sure nuff."

"Just you pack that alien stuff in there, Wayne Bob. This here is a *Royal Space Force* moke. Filled to the sills with cucumber sandwiches and English muffins, I reckon."

"It's on the stolen list and you know it", said the second voice sulkily. "Besides, what killed her driver, you tell me that iffen you can."

"We've no proof the driver *is* dead, Wayne Bob." A head and a pair of hands emerged into the saucer. The head was human. It was the head of a white man with a flat-topped haircut. He winked at Ant.

"Well, what have we here. The RSF is training midgets as pilots to reduce payload weight. Gimme some thrust in here, Wayne Bob, I don't hold with this Free Fall stuff."

The deck around Ant rumbled gently, and all the debris in the air fell to the floor. Ant felt himself drift gently down with it.

"The gravity's back", whispered Cleo. "What did they do?"

"Fired their engines, most likely", Ant whispered back. "It's not real gravity - it's caused by acceleration, like the feel of the seat pressing against your back when you take off in a plane." He kicked himself mentally. "Of course! That's why we had gravity for the trip out here. Our engines were turned on."

"Why did the gravity go off halfway through the trip, then?"

"The ship stopped accelerating forwards and started decelerating. Spaceships don't brake like cars. It takes them a long time to stop."

Billy Hank rolled down into the cabin. He was moving like a moonman - gravity was still feeble.

The American spaceman held a torch, which he played round the cabin.

"Your average human stomach contains a deal of hydrochloric acid, I reckon", observed Billy Hank. "Been a whole lot of barfing going on in here, Wayne Bob."

"Smells like the inside of a diaper", agreed Wayne Bob.

"What's a diaper?" said Cleo.

"Real purdy find", continued Wayne Bob, without replying to Cleo. His head was now in the cabin too; it suffered from a severe lack of teeth. Both he and Billy Hank were wearing flight suits with a number, '12A', on the left breast. "Astromoke Mark Three, if my eyes do not deceive me, in perfect working order."

"These British copies ain't quite so good", said Billy Hank. "Don't got no poke over a standing quarter light year."

The torch swung round to shine right in Ant and Cleo's eyes.

"You kids are in more trouble than a male Black Widow spider in sweet, sweet love."

5 - Too Many Moons

There were too many moons, the sky was the wrong colour, and it was cold.

Ant had expected some sort of huge futuristic space terminal. Instead, the ship had dropped out of a sky the colour of strawberry custard onto a landscape that had at first appeared dead, and had then, as the ground came closer, seemed covered with dead woodland. Finally, once they were skimming almost at treetop height, he had seen that there were leaves on many of the dead trees.

"It's sunset here", said Ant. "And autumn."

Billy Hank shook his head. "Plants here don't use none of - what's that there chemical that your fancy Earth undergrowth uses fer photosynthesizin'?"

"Chlorophyll", said Cleo.

"Yup. That green un. Don't got us none o'that here. All our plants are brown. Way it should be", he added proudly, tapping a plaque on the wall that said WELCOME TO THE LAND OF THE LONG AUTUMN.

The ship, which Ant had been proudly informed was the USASF Corvette *Virginia,* skipped and dipped over the landscape until it finally stopped almost dead in the air above a flat-topped rocky outcrop barely the size of a school playing field. There were a few dish aerials and refuelling tanks scattered here and there. Despite the fact that it seemed to behave more like a helicopter than an aeroplane, the ship ploughed a furrow in the ground with its skids when it landed. Billy Hank looked at Wayne Bob severely.

There was an American flag flapping dispiritedly in the breeze. Although it was an American flag, however, it was not the *right* American flag.

"That's not an American flag", Ant whispered to Cleo. "That's an X with stars on it."

"It's not the Stars and Stripes. It's the *Confederate* flag,", replied Cleo; and she sounded worried.

"What's so bad about a flag?" said Ant.

"Would you feel good if the flag had a swastika on it?"

What does she mean by that? thought Ant - but then there was far too much else to think about.

"I don't think these are real Americans", he whispered quietly to her. "They're some sort of American space morons."

Then, they were hustled inside, into an office that was only partially built above ground level. Ant had not even known it was an office, as earth was piled up around its walls, and it looked more like a hillock; Billy Hank and Wayne Bob had to lead them right around it before they could see the entrance, a door down a flight of metal steps. The office was filled with wires and circuit boards and bits of flying saucer. There were two chairs, and a table, keyboard and screen that Ant imagined must operate some sort of air traffic control system, and, ominously, a rack of guns - the same sort of gun their kidnapper had waved at them. As there were only two chairs, Ant and Cleo were forced to sit on ammunition crates. There were many ammunition crates.

Ant felt weird and giddy, as if he were somehow sitting on a roller coaster whilst at the same time sitting on an ammunition crate without moving.

"Look, we aren't anything to do with him", said Ant, nodding at the still unconscious pilot of their saucer, who lay on the floor, breathing heavily and sweating.

"He *kidnapped* us", said Cleo. "He pointed a *gun* at us."

"This gun?" said Billy Hank, holding up the horribly large pistol the saucer pilot had threatened them with. "Now, child, you can't know a deal about firearms if you don't know when one of 'em ain't loaded." He tilted the pistol grip of the weapon up to Cleo's eyes. It was empty.

"Hey!" shouted Wayne Bob, as if he'd only just noticed this, "this wun's a Nigger."

To do her credit, Cleo didn't even blink. Instead, she simply said:

"I'm sorry, I don't understand that word. Could it be that it is a word used on your planet to describe black people? On my planet, you see, there is no race prejudice and we all live happily in harmony."

Wayne Bob gave a shudder, as if Cleo had described his own personal version of Hell. And then Billy Hank, who had seemed the kindlier of the two up to this point, said to Ant:

"You got to understand, we do things different here. You're in the town of Croatoan, the one and only settlement on the planet of New Dixie."

Ant blinked. "You and Wayne Bob are a *town*?"

"Don't give me no sass there, boy. This here's a Christian city of over two hundred souls."

Ant looked out of the window and saw only sand blowing in the wind. "There's nobody out there", he said gently.

"All underground", said Billy Hank. "Can't rightly live on the surface, on account of the heat and the cold and the tides and the fungal parasites and aboriginal megafauna."

"Sounds nice", said Ant, wondering what an aboriginal megafauna was and whether it had anything to do with Australia.

"Where *are* we?" said Cleo; and then, as if the two men had been trying to convince her otherwise, said: "This is *not* Northamptonshire."

Billy Hank bent down to Cleo's level. "Pretty little monkey, ain't she, Wayne Bob? Where you from, child?"

"Africa", said Cleo, although Ant knew perfectly well she had been born in Chatham.

"That's on Earth, ain't it?" Billy Hank looked to Wayne Bob for confirmation. Wayne Bob nodded.

"Well, child", continued Billy Hank, "you are on one of five planets orbiting Barnard's Star, six light years from Earth."

Cleo swallowed.

"That means I'm not going to be home in time for tea, doesn't it."

Billy Hank grinned and roughed up Cleo's carefully arranged hair extensions. "Your nigra friend'll be given some easy manual labour. You, on the other hand, young man, will have to go to School."

"Crikey", said Ant. "I wish *I* was a negro."

Wayne Bob and Billy Hank looked at him sternly.

***

The classroom was hot. Everywhere below ground was hot. This was, Ant had been told, because it was difficult to pump the air around to recirculate it. Something called 'Sheet Fungus' kept growing on the air filters in the pumps. The desk Ant was working at was made of wood so old and worm-eaten that it was spongy to the touch. It had the names of many previous occupants carved into it. Most of them appeared to have been called Glenn. Outside the classroom - which was a cubic space carved into solid rock and lined with plastic boards - someone was squeaking a mop up and down the dusty corridor. The corridor, Ant knew, was dusty because its walls, floor and ceiling were made of earth.

Ant's schoolmates all had hair a millimetre in length (in the case of the boys) and twined severely into pigtails (in the case of the girls). They were very noticeably all white. There was a school uniform; a powder-blue, military style thing which had the number '12A' on the left breast, and which involved Ant wearing shorts. Ant's classmates marvelled at his tanned brown legs.

The teacher was writing on the blackboard with a stick of what should have been chalk, and was instead some other mineral that kept breaking and scarring the board. What she had written so far said CROATOAN - OUR TOWN ITS HISTORY. Nobody in the entire room seemed to be interested apart from Ant, who wanted desperately to know how an entire town of American rednecks had ended up orbiting Barnard's Star.

"We begin our story", said the teacher, "in the year 1947. America had emerged from the Second World War as the most powerful nation in the world."

There was a chorus of yee-haws and hooooowhees from the audience, and the teacher waited for the patriotism to subside.

"Without America's assistance", said the teacher, "the ancient and more decadent nations of the Old World would have been engulfed by the menace of Nazzyism under Aydolf Hitler. Only America stood firm against the onslaught of Nazzy Germany, declaring war after Hitler invaded Poland. Hitler's less brave European neighbours only dared to enter the war after the American victories at the Battle of D-Day."

Ant put up his hand. Outside, the mop continued to squeak.

"Isn't it *actually* true that the Americans entered the war two years after everyone else, and sustained hardly any casualties in comparison to the British, Russians and Chinese?"

The teacher squinted at Ant.

"You're the little Earth boy, aren't you."

"Sure am, ma'am", said Ant.

"Well, Anthony, you are going to have to learn that we don't interrupt our teachers on New Dixie."

Ant put his hand down and mumbled, "Sorry, ma'am."

The teacher continued. "America was the most technologically sophisticated nation in the world, the most democratic, the most free. However, several evils remained to be fought." She scribbled in four more lines, which were:

COMMUNISM

INTER RACIAL MIXING

TWO TONE MUSIC

WOOLLY THINKING

"Even with the great strength that had been given it by God, America had a powerful fight on its hands. However, heaven had another gift to give. In the year 1947", said the teacher, writing up the date on the board, "three air force interceptors were engaged by an alien craft in the desert in New Mexico, and destroyed it in a dogfight."

Ant could remember his father watching a documentary on TV in which earnest men in T shirts, beards and sandals had explained how an Unidentified Flying Object had crashed near a town in New Mexico, and how the American government had hushed up the whole affair, and that the town was called -

"Roswell", breathed Ant.

"Precisely, Anthony." The teacher actually smiled. "I can see you know your history. Such was the technological sophistication of the craft that it took many years before the advanced techniques involved in constructing her could be simulated. The programme was highly secret and expensive, and not even known by the President."

Ant put up his hand.

"Yes, Stevens?"

"Pardon me, ma'am, but if the President was supposed to run the country, and he didn't know what the military were doing, how could the country have been called democratic or free?"

The teacher stared at Ant as if attempting to force him to explode by sheer force of glare power.

"Go to the back of the room and face the corner", she said.

The class giggled. Ant rose, and rose to go.

"And wear this", she said, lifting something from her desk and handing it to Ant. It was a white plastic cone, with a large black letter 'D' written on it.

"D", said the teacher with immense satisfaction, "for Dunce."

The class laughed again. This audience, it seemed, would laugh at anything. Outside, the mop was lifted and wrung out, then filled with water again and set to squeaking on the floor once more.

The teacher continued her lesson.

"America's first interstellar vehicle, the *Explorator*, flew in 1951 and reconnoitred Alpha Centauri, immediately discovering the habitable planets which go round, or *orbit,* that star. America's first colonies were founded not long afterwards. It was not long after that that America began to hand down its knowledge of interstellar flight to less *fortunate* races, such as the British."

The class giggled again. Ant's ears burned.

"It was at this point, however, that our glorious nation fell under attack again - not from outside, but from within.

"Those who planned America's interstellar colonies did so secretly, knowing that dark forces were afoot in the very centres of American power themselves. Pernicious African rock and roll music, white liberalism and a refusal of the negro to respect his proper place made America so weak by the 1970's that she was defeated on the battlefield by a tiny nation of Communists in South East Asia -"

There were more sniggers, and someone said: "Anthony got him brown nigger legs. He a nigger."

Then a girl, a white-skinned, blonde girl with regulation pigtails, put her hand up, and asked: "Miss Ikeman, is *Anthony* a negro?"

Miss Ikeman laughed. "Good heavens no, child. It's just that he's been up outside, under the Sun of Earth. That Sun is even brighter and whiter than corridor lighting, rather than the proper dim red colour of sunlight *we* are used to. Earth's sun shines with a stronger ultraviolet light, and tans the skin. Anthony has over-exposed himself and will of course probably suffer from skin cancer in later life, like most inhabitants of Earth who are foolish enough to go outdoors."

Whispers circulated round the class, and "He's been *Outside*" seemed to be whispered, if anything, with greater disbelief than "He's from *Earth.*"

Then Miss Ikeman opened the door to the classroom, and what Ant had been dreading happened. She walked back in with Cleo, dragging her by the arm. Cleo's hair had been done up in what was obviously intended to look like a bandana, and she had a mop and bucket in her hands.

"Now *this*, children", said Miss Ikeman, "is a Negro. Observe the slouching stance, the pouting, arrogant demeanour, and - saints alive! The violent tendencies." Cleo had only stamped her foot, but Miss Ikeman had jumped as if electrified.

Miss Ikeman caught hold of Cleo's arm with a grip of iron. Cleo winced. "Y'all can all see", she said, "the smaller skull, containing the less advanced negro brain."

Cleo's skull did not look any smaller, from Ant's viewpoint, than Miss Ikeman's. Her lip was also beginning to tremble.

In a moment of inspiration, Ant whipped off his dunce's cap, whirled round and popped it on Miss Ikeman's head. The white plastic fell over her eyes, blocking her vision.

"OBSERVE", yelled Ant to the class, "THE SMALL SKULL, CONTAINING THE LESS ADVANCED BRAIN."

Miss Ikeman screeched, turned around, and ran full tilt into the wall. The class screamed, but it was a scream of laughter. Ant had the impression they had not been entertained so well in ages. They crowded round the door, watching Miss Ikeman run down the electrically-lit corridor outside, bumping into the wall, whimpering and attempting frantically to rip the plastic cone from off her head.

Cleo turned to Ant.

"I wasn't going to cry", she said. "But thanks."

"I knew you weren't", said Ant. "No thanks are necessary." And then, bending over closer and whispering more quietly, he said:

"*Don't worry. We are getting out of here. I promise.*"

***

"This here's your new family", said Billy Hank.

"I've already got a family, thanks", said Ant frostily. *Though I only see half of it at any one time*, he added to himself.

The room didn't look too different from any normal living room, apart from the fact that it was so small. It was a friendly room - insanely friendly, with big happy teddy bears, clowns and golliwogs painted inexpertly on the walls. Ant had never trusted clowns, and decided to disapprove of the golliwogs as a point of loyalty to Cleo. The room also had no windows. It had no windows because what was behind the walls painted with clowns and golliwogs was many, many metres of solid rock.

There was also a lock on the door.

"But your old family are *communists*", said Draylene. Draylene, as far as Ant could work out, was the woman Billy Hank and Wayne Bob had decided should be his new mother. She had teeth that splayed out in different directions, and eyes to match.

"My father", said Ant, "is *not* a communist." *Which is true, after all. He's just a rabid trades unionist who buys diesel oil from terrorists.*

"We understand", said Jesse Clem. Jesse Clem was kindly and unsettling. His trousers were pulled up till the waist sat just below his nipples. "You done been brainwashed there. But we'll keep your brain nice and clean here, oh yes we will. You got to realise, son, that your *entire family* are communists. Except *you*, now, that is. You're safe here with us, oh yes you are." He put his hand on Ant's shoulder. It was very heavy.

"You done got you a little brother now too", said Draylene. She stood aside in the doorway, and a hideous three-foot goblin came in. It was red-haired, covered in freckles, and had inherited its mother's teeth. Ant knew instinctively that women would find it adorable.

It stared at Ant.

"Am goan kill yew", it said, and ran out making Red Indian war whoops.

"That there's your little brother Billy Jed", said Jesse Clem. "Ain't he a scamp?"

Billy Hank pointed at the bed in the corner, which had a handmade quilt covered in still more bears. "That's your bunk there." He bent down closer to Ant and whispered in his ear. *"Now, Draylene and Jesse Clem here just lost them their youngest, little Jimmy Brad, to the Swamp Fever. Iffen they don't got two children, they don't qualify for quarters of this size no more, you hear? Now you be good to these folks, and I'll be good to you."*

6 - Naming of Parts

"NOW, THIS AFTERNOON, BOYS", said the big strong man at the front of the room, "AS IS ESSENTIAL IN ANY SOCIETY THAT AIMS TO MAKE ITSELF READY FOR THE THREATS POSED BY COMMUNISM AND INTERNATIONAL NEGRITUDE, WE ARE GOING TO LEARN THE PROPER CARE AND HANDLING OF FIREARMS."

He stopped to let the Yeehaws subside, and turned to lift one of the massive weapons out of the gun rack to his left. It looked too large even for a grown-up to use. Ant watched reproachfully from the back of the room. Initially, when he'd been told the afternoon's classes were Hunting, Shooting and Crawdad Fishing, he'd been excited. However, the morning's incident with the plastic cone and Miss Ikeman's head had led to a meeting with the Principal in which he'd been forbidden to handle firearms until further notice.

He observed Sergeant Sheldrake carrying out the field stripping and cleaning of the MX1000A GyroEagle rocket rifle sulkily.

"YOU, Mr. Stevens", roared Sergeant Sheldrake suddenly, jabbing a sausage-thick finger in Ant's direction. "What is the purpose of the Side Exhaust Release Valve?"

Ant thought fast. "Erm - to release exhaust at the side?"

"Aha, so you *was* listening, boy. Continue to do thusly. Now, if we unscrew the top inspection plate *here,* we can see the main striking plate for the rocket exhaust gases -"

Still, Ant, thought, it couldn't be too bad. Tomorrow was a class called 'Astromoke Care', which sounded promisingly like being taught to maintain a flying saucer.

One of the boys in the row in front of Ant turned round and said, out of the corner of his mouth:

"Miss Ikeman got her the rest of the week off lying down. Now we got Principal Prickett for Gunplay and Political Orientation, and we can git him to talk about Plane Geometry for *hours*."

"That sounds dire", said Ant.

"Oh no", said the boy quickly, "it's real sweet. Some of us just hate having to learn to fly spaceships and shoot guns and stuff." He pulled open a page of his exercise book and showed Ant a drawing which had GLENN BOB DRAWED THIS written at the top of it. "It's an Isosceles Triangle", he confided.

"And an Equilateral one, too, by the look of it", whispered Ant.

"Do you know anything about Pythagoras?" said Glenn Bob urgently.

"Well", said Ant conspiratorially, "I've heard that the square on the hypotenuse is equal to the sum of the squares on the other two sides."

Glenn Bob whistled. "Hooeee! Don't that just beat all!"

Where Cleo was, Ant had no idea. However, if he could learn how to use a gun *and* fly an Astromoke, Ant reasoned the two of them could steal a saucer and fly away to Earth.

"Can *you* fly a *spaceship*?" he said to Glenn Bob. The other boy reddened. "No. We ain't got to that lesson yet. Maintainin a Moke in Level Flight is right plumb at the back of the book, and Landin and Take Off are next year's syllabus."

"What about interstellar navigation?"

"Oh, you got to be in the graduate class afore you can do *that*."

"How long does that take?"

"Seven year."

Ant slumped down into his seat, defeated.

***

Cleo, meanwhile, was scrubbing a floor. She had divided the floor into sections, of which she had completed eleven sixteenths.

Cleo's grandmother had scrubbed floors when she had first come to Britain from the West Indies. Her grandmother had told her that, when you started dividing the floor down into the bits you'd done and the bits you hadn't done, you were starting to let the job get to you. Cleo had started by dividing the floor in two, so that she could feel good after she'd finished half of it. Then she'd divided it in four, so that she could feel a sense of achievement in half the time. Then had come eight, and finally sixteen, and thirty two was a distinct possibility in the near future.

"Still", she told herself, "look on the bright side. It'll teach you binary mathematics. You can be a genius computer programmer when you leave school."

"*If* you ever leave school", she added as she looked up at the metal pipes that snaked across the earth ceiling above her.

It was not too bad, working as a skivvy for the Croatoan folk. Most of them had never actually seen a black person, and consequently, although they *tried* to be racist, they didn't know what to say. People from Cleo's own home town in England could be far crueller. These people called her 'little monkey' and 'little piccaninny', which sounded positively sweet compared to what she got called at home.

"You finished that floor yet, li'l bush baby?" came the voice of Miss Maybelline, the Domestic Cleanliness Supervisor.

"Nearly plumb three quarter finished, Miss Mae", she trilled back.

Cleo was also beginning to realise that Croatoan was dying.

The people of the town all seemed to suffer from illnesses of one kind or another - the children were pale because they never set foot above ground, the adults had rickety limbs and bleeding gums. The community was probably not able to feed itself properly. And everything technological, everywhere in the rats' nest of tunnels, kept on breaking down. The whole town went into fits of rejoicing every time a ship arrived from any other world carrying spare parts, medicine, or food. And the corridors were filthy, even here, outside the door to the medical bay.

Cleo suddenly realised, as she peered into the hospital area, that she could see the saucer pilot who had kidnapped her, lying on a bed - possibly the *only* bed. He was no longer breathing and sweating heavily, and seemed to be sleeping peacefully. There were, however, canvas bands tied around his bunk to stop him leaving it if he woke up.

Cleo tiptoed into the medical bay, being careful not to leave marks on the floor. The man was actually quite handsome for a kidnapper, if you ignored his military haircut. He hadn't been shaved in several days, and was growing the beginnings of a beard. A plastic board fastened to the foot of his bed said: TURPIN, R., 63, PRISONER OF WAR, BULLET TRAUMA, MORPHINE TWICE DAILY.

"So you're not one of them", she said. "And you're a soldier. Where are you from, then?" She reached up to the man's throat, and felt around his collar. Just as she'd thought, a metal dog tag on a chain was hung round the man's throat. It said TURPIN, R., 63.

"Wherever you're from", she said, "they can't have many soldiers if you're only number sixty-three. Why couldn't you have been useful for something? All you do is lie on your back *breathing*. We're trapped here because of you. Can't you do *anything*?"

M. Turpin, 63, didn't answer. Miss Maybelline was calling again. Silently, Cleo picked up her bucket and mop and tiptoed out of the hospital.

***

"The Colonies of the United States of America in space", said Principal Prickett, "originally numbered thirteen - New New York, Newer England, Novior Scotia, Nueva California, Mas Nuevo Mexico, La Plus Nouvelle Orléans, Nixon, New Nebraska, Louisiana Nova, Hawaii Hou, Novaya Alyeska, Brand Spanking New Hampshire, and our own proud homeland of New Dixie.

"It has been said", said Principal Prickett, who had a weirdly fascinating huge mole with a hair on it growing out of his left cheek, "that the number thirteen is unlucky, particularly considering the devastating rebellion that also ended the Thirteen Colonies of the British in the New World." He nodded to Ant, probably because Ant was the only person in the room listening. "Therefore, our colony has been numbered 12A, a number we wear with pride." He thumped his own badge vigorously.

"Our colonies have already suffered rebellion, however. Not good, honest rebellion of the sort that formed our great country to begin with, but mean, despicable rebellion fomented by Communist degenerates." And on his next overhead projector slide, he actually did have a picture of a communist degenerate, who resembled Ant's dad.

"In 1974, our original thirteen colonies turned renegade, proclaiming themselves the 'United States of the Zodiac'", said Principal Prickett. "We took one of those colonies back, and it is only a matter of time before our forces re-take the other twelve. Propaganda fed to USZ citizens leads them to believe that they live in a starry-eyed Utopia, where one man casts one vote, each citizen is allowed his or her opinion, and there is always enough food to eat." The Principal's next slide had a painting of a happy family, who were presumably USZ citizens, tucking in to a hearty meal of some roast animal or other which appeared to have six legs. This slide was, perhaps, unwise. Some of the thinner boys and girls in the class were staring at the screen as if they might jump up and attempt to eat it.

"POPPYCOCK!" yelled the Principal, throwing a book at a particularly emaciated boy in the second row. "Stop dribbling, boy! For *this* is the *real* story."

He wound on to the next slide, which showed a dejected group of sallow-cheeked people trudging through the ruins of what had once been a colony resembling Croatoan. It took Ant several seconds to realise that the group in the second painting were the family from the first.

"Starvation! Continual civil war! Rivers running with blood! Plagues of locusts!" The Principal was pointing at each of these evils as he spoke, which had actually been drawn in by the artist. Ant was not convinced. He put up a hand.

"Yes, boy."

"These United States of the Zodiac. Might they have enemies and agents even here, in our midst, sir?"

The Principal stared at Ant with great suspicion. "Sure as death and taxes, Mr. Stevens."

"Then how do they communicate with their degenerate Communist masters?"

Glenn Bob turned round in his chair. "That's easy. All their ships use the same frequency. You can listen in on them iffen you got an Electric Wireless that receives on 100 kilohertz - "

"DON'T give out information to a potential Agent of Communism, boy!" thundered Principal Prickett. "This here pupil is still on Probation."

Glenn Bob turned back round in his chair, eyes front.

"Tomorrow", said Principal Prickett, "we shall be going Outside."

The class was silent, save for a chorus of amazed whispers.

"Yes, you heard me right", said the Principal. "Having assessed the worthiness of this class over the past few months, I am convinced that it exhibits the gumption and frontier spirit necessary to survive the rigours of the Out-Of-Doors. We are going outside the colony perimeter on an excursion to devegetate our perimeter - specifically, a section of our protective electric fence, which has been shut down specially for the occasion. Sergeant Sheldrake will be present with a weapon at all times, and if the weather is fair, we may go skinny dipping and crawdad fishing."

The class shivered with dread. Ant leaned forward and whispered:

"What's Devegetating our Perimeter?"

"Weedin'", said Glenn Bob.

"Skinny dipping sounds good", said Ant.

"Water's five degrees above freezin'", said Glenn Bob. "And there's crawdads."

"What's a crawdad? Isn't it some sort of little freshwater shrimp thing?"

Glenn Bob turned round in his chair and favoured Ant with a particularly unpleasant stare.

"Ours are about horse size", he said.

7 - Roanoke

"You took *ages*", hollered Cleo. "Where've you been?"

Ant stepped out from behind a mass of pipes labelled:

NO.3 DETRITUS PUMP

LOOK OUT

EXTREME DANGER

THERE

HUMAN WASTE

Y'ALL

"Class just ended", bellowed Ant. "Principal Prickett got excited about the Right to Bear Arms, and we had to stay in another twenty minutes." He stared at the sign on the pump. "Did we have to meet in a sewer?"

"This here ain't no sewer", yelled Cleo, imitating Miss Maybelline perfectly. "This here is a *Waste Recycling Facility*. Don't get the wrong end of the stick there, y'all." She collapsed giggling.

The rumbling of the pipes subsided slightly, and Ant could hear himself think, just barely. What he heard himself thinking was *try not to lean on anything.* "How did you get time off work?"

"I skive off whenever I want. It's great. Miss Maybelline expects me to be lazy. All her books say black people are lazy. If I start working hard she gets worried. It sends her into agonies of self-doubt."

"I found out some useful stuff."

"So did I. Our Mr. Turpin is being held in the sickbay near Airlock Thirteen."

"Who's Mr. Turpin?"

"That's his name. Our Flying Saucer pilot. They're keeping him under sedation. He rolls over and dribbles occasionally. He's a Prisoner of War."

"Ah!" said Ant, with a vast air of knowledge. "He'll be from the USZ, then."

"The *what*, now?"

"The United States of the Zodiac. They're a sort of rebel American colony in space. Principal Prickett spent two whole hours this afternoon trying to convince me to hate them, so I figure they're probably all right. All we need is a radio that transmits on 100 kilohertz, and we can get in contact with them."

"They're very careful about radios that transmit on *any* frequency", said Cleo. "I had to clean the general stores this afternoon, and all the radio transmitters are kept in a big locked room at one end along with the guns and the keys to the saucers -"

Suddenly, she broke off.

"Did you hear that?"

"I didn't hear anything but humming", said Ant.

"The humming changed", said Cleo, staring round the chamber with the quiet paranoia of a pussy cat.

"Maybe someone in the colony went to the toilet", said Ant.

Cleo padded round the rows of pipes and softly rumbling machinery. "It changed a *lot.*"

"Maybe they went to the toilet a lot."

"Aha!" Cleo suddenly became a blur of arms and hair extensions. "GOTCHA!"

"OW!" yelled a patch of darkness, and then: "Uncle! UNCLE!"

"WHERE's your uncle?" yelled Cleo. "Don't you DARE yell for your uncle."

"I think he means 'stop squeezing the end of my nose like a juiced lemon', Cleo", said Ant. "Besides, I know him. His name's Glenn Bob. He's a friend."

"Oh, you have *friends* among these barbarians, do you?" said Cleo with surprising venom. "Hello, *friend.*"

"'lo", said Glenn Bob meekly, and then: "I knowed you was up to no good when you started askin about radio frequencies." He rubbed his face gingerly. "I done got my face twisted by a nigger. Is my nose brown?"

Cleo's face took only a half second to transform into a huge theatrical smile. "What makes you think we're up to no good, Robert? We're only talking together as two old friends do."

"Ma name's Bob", said Glenn Bob. "An you was talkin about radio transceivers. Ain't no-one allowed to talk about radio transceivers without they got permission from the Governor."

Then his face brightened a little and he said: "I know where there is some, iffen that'll help any."

Cleo's eyes became huge. "*You*? Help *us*? Why would you want to do that?"

Glenn Bob stared hard at the floor. "Well", he said, "my pa's one of the town MP's -"

"I didn't think you had MP's in America", said Ant. "I thought you had senators."

"I don't think he means Members of Parliament", said Cleo. "I think he means *Military Policemen.* This place is run like a giant military camp, remember? I've seen them swanking around the corridors. Big men, about gorilla size, with guns to match."

Glenn Bob nodded. "My pa leaves his gun belt on his uniform pants when he goes to bed, and we ain't allowed to touch it. I stole one of the bullets an hid it in my brother Bobby Glenn's pocket an it went through the auto-mangle in the town laundromat. It shot old Ma Knickerbocker's knickerbockers full of holes, an set light to fifteen complete ensemblies."

"What's an ensembly?" said Ant, who was not female.

"A complete suit of clothes", said Cleo, who was.

"Golly gee", said Glenn Bob, gaping at the awesome extent of his misdeed. "I didn't know that. No wonder pa was mad. I thought it was some sort of big handkerchief."

"'Ensemble' comes from the French word *ensemble*", added Cleo. "Meaning 'an ensemble', she added.

"So I'm plumb bound to get my ass whupped for sure", finished Glenn Bob.

"I see", said Ant. "And that's a bad thing, is it?"

Glenn Bob nodded. "I'm fixin to run away from home", he said.

"So where's the radio transmitter?" said Ant.

"Roanoke", said Glenn Bob. "Site of the first colony. The first colonists was craziern a one-legged rattlesnake with its legs crossed. Whatever a rattlesnake is", he added. "I ain't never seen one."

"Why were they crazy?" said Cleo.

"They set up camp in the lowlands, right down there with the megafauna and the humptybacked decapods and the vampire hellbenders", said Glenn Bob..

"Sounds nice", said Cleo. "And they'll let us use this radio transmitter, will they?"

Glenn Bob's face lit up. "That's the beauty of it. They ain't around to ask! The hellbenders and the fungus got 'em, every one."

"I see", said Ant. "And this makes you think that Roanoke would be a good place to visit."

"Safe as anywhere else in the lowlands. Anyways", said Glenn Bob, "we'll only be there but a while, till you can call up one of they Rebel Space Cruisers of yourn and get us out of there, right?" He looked from Ant to Cleo. "Right?"

"Riiiight", said Ant, nodding slowly. "I mean", he said, suddenly starting to nod confidently and vigorously, "right, eh, Cleo?"

"Oh, absolutely. Anything you boys say. Who am I to object to being vampirised and hellbent."

***

They watched Glenn Bob leave from behind a mass of valves.

"I have grave reservations about this, Ant", said Cleo.

"I'm not happy either", said Ant. "But he heard everything we said. We've got to let him come with us."

"I'm going to have to get out of town unnoticed."

"Cleo, you're allowed in every single corridor in town. You *clean* every single corridor in town. How is it going to be difficult for you to get out of town unnoticed?"

"With an inflatable dinghy, compass, food, packs, oars, three changes of shoes, cold weather clothing, guns, and a clear and concise map of the area?" said Cleo. "And a whistle for attracting attention?"

"Eh?" said Ant.

"You're really not very organised, are you? How long do you think we'll survive out there without a whistle?"

"We don't need three changes of shoes, Cleo."

Cleo frowned sulkily.

"Besides, how are you going to get hold of any of that stuff?"

"TADAAA!" Cleo held up something between finger and thumb. It jangled.

"And what is that?"

"Only the set of spare keys to the main town stores, which I cleaned, vacuumed and blackleaded yesterday."

Ant whistled. "Hooooeeee!"

"What part of the perimeter are you going to be devegetating tomorrow?"

"Airlock twelve", said Ant. "I don't know where that is. They don't allow me maps in case I'm a spy. They blacked out all the maps in my geography textbook."

"Airlock twelve is just between the under eights' firing range and the indoor hydroponic cotton field", said Cleo. "I had to mop up the blood in the one and pick half a ton of cotton in the other. They've got an automatic robot cotton picking machine which they amusingly call a 'RoboNegro 2000'. It breaks down." She breathed on her fingers and scored up a point for herself in the air. "Ain't no substitute for the real thing."

Ant looked at Cleo nervously. "Cleo, you sound as if you're growing to like it."

Cleo stared hard at Ant. "Well, let me disillusion you. I do not like it. I do not like it one little bit. Today Miss Maybelline made an off-the-cuff comment about getting the MP's to whup me if I didn't work faster. *And I don't think she was joking.*"

"Okay, okay. We're getting out of here. Keep your bandana on. I've got to go home to my family now. Ma Williamson's making roast beef and Yorkshire pudding without any roast beef or Yorkshire pudding as a special treat because I'm English."

Cleo wrinkled up her nose. "Sounds lovely."

"What are your family like?"

"I have to do the dishes, iron the laundry, change the baby, and clean the floor every time Jimmy Earl Junior runs in mud all over it, which he does every ten minutes to get me in trouble. I have to get out of here, Ant."

"Don't worry. We are leaving."

8 - Outside

The airlock door was operated by Sergeant Sheldrake, who wound it open using sheer muscle power and a wheel mounted next to the door, labelled MANUAL OVERRIDE. This, to Ant, suggested that the door had originally been electrically operated, which in turn suggested that the electricity had long since failed. While he wound the wheel, Sergeant Sheldrake kept an anxious eye on the world outside the door he was opening.

The door was made of steel, thick as a brick. It had dents and scratches in its outside surface. Luckily there was no sign outside of whatever had made the scratches; only a jumble of enormous rocks covered with what looked and smelt like dead stinking seaweed. Ant, who had been expecting a rush of fresh air when the door opened, ground his teeth together in frustration.

"Stick to the path", said Sergeant Sheldrake. "Do not touch anything, no matter how pink and fluffy it appears. I am thinking particularly here of those of you of the female persuasion."

What the Sergeant could have meant by that, Ant had no idea - until, a few steps out into the reeking air, they passed a rock wall covered with what looked for all the world like fluffy pink pencil cases of the sort small girls would fight to possess. No girl, without being warned, could have resisted reaching out to pet them, and possibly even insert pencils into them, an action which would almost certainly have resulted in the creatures attempting to defend themselves.

"Jackson's Deadly Carmine Sea Puff", said Sergeant Sheldrake with gruff respect. "They get stranded here at high tide. Their plush pink envenomed integuments will despatch a fully grown Rebel prisoner of war in under a minute."

Ant wondered briefly how Sergeant Sheldrake got such information - but secretly, he knew the answer, even if he was not sure he wanted to. And this information led him inevitably to the conclusion: *When our own Rebel prisoner of war, Mr. Turpin, is fit to leave the hospital, what will happen to him then?*

He pulled his wrist up close to his mouth and, pretending to look at his watch, hissed:

"Rude Dog to Princess Meow, I think we have a problem, over."

Around his wrist, a tiny radio communicator that had been carefully stolen by Cleo buzzed back: *"Princess Meow to Rude Dog, we are approaching Location Thunderzord with The Goods, it had better be a damn good problem, over."*

"Am approaching Location Thunderzord myself, but our problem is Mr. Turpin. I think if he stays here he's going to die, Cleo, over."

"I'm Princess Meow, not Cleo, idiot. Everyone with a functioning wrist communicator now knows who I am, over -"

Glenn Bob leaned over to Ant. "She's quite right there, actually", he said.

"NO - TALKIN - IN - LINE." Sergeant Sheldrake picked up Ant and Glenn Bob, with one hand on the scruff of each of their uniform collars, and marched them to the front of the line. *Great*, thought Ant. *Now we've no chance of getting away.*

"On your LEFT" (went Sergeant Sheldrake's running commentary, his hand fixed on Ant's shoulder like a ten ton parrot) "is what appears to the untutored eye to be a beautiful blue rock pool." Ant took Sergeant Sheldrake's word for it. In the red light from the sky, all things were varying shades of scarlet. The Carmine Sea Puffs might actually have looked white in Earth sunlight.

Why, Ant thought to himself, *does everything at ground level on this planet look like it belongs on a beach at low tide?*

Sergeant Sheldrake pulled a pinch of tofu jerky from his pocket and tossed it into the pool. The pool walls closed like a camera shutter, splattering pool water over the nearby rocks where it steamed and sizzled like eggs frying on a hot griddle. Where the pool had been was now a boulder-sized mass heaving like a whole kennel of dogs fighting in a sack.

"That is the above-ground stomach of a Spivey's Common Nibbler", said the Sergeant. "Had that been your leg in there, it'd've been a long hop home. The first sign of the presence of a Nibbler is the wonderful clear blueness of the water. This is on account of the fact that Nibbler stomach juices contain sulphuric acid. It is not pond water y'all are observing. It is bile."

How do these people live *on such a planet*, thought Ant, and then reminded himself that, of course, they didn't. They cowered underground and hid from the planet instead.

"Of course, the *really* dangerous critters are excluded by our Electrified Perimeter", drawled the Sergeant. "Hence the reason for our excursion, ladies."

Sheldrake had now stopped in front of a heap of gloves, masks, kneeling pads, and shovels.

"You *will* use the gloves; you *will* wear the kneeling pads; you *will* wear a mask. If you do not and one of the weeds bites you, chances are you might not make it back to sickbay."

Bites you? thought Ant.

The gloves were of tough, scratchy material, and reached up to Ant's elbows. The masks were so heavily pitted and scratched as to make wearing them like seeing the world through a toilet window. The shovel had seen better days. With the kneepads strapped on together as well, Ant felt like a cricketer going out to bat.

The perimeter fence was the most impressive item of engineering Ant had seen on New Dixie. It was twice the height of a house, supported on immense concrete pillars and strung with cable stretched taut up to the top, where coils of rusty barbed wire were tangled. The taut wires, Ant guessed, would be the electrified ones.

The Sergeant threw a shovel against the fence. It bounced off without being electrified.

"Current's off", he said. "Get to work."

He propped himself on a high boulder out of the way of the wind, and scanned the terrain outside the fence nervously. Ant noted that his hands were still round the trigger and foregrip of his rifle.

How do I get out of this? thought Ant. *I can't run away from here to Airlock Thirteen without being missed, and this is the only part of the perimeter where the current in the wire's switched off. How are we going to escape all together,* with *Mr. Turpin,* and *get through the wire?*

Devegetation turned out to be back-breaking work. The rocks were covered with a dense thatch of what Sergeant Sheldrake described as 'Charybdis's Hair', a slippery, oily plant that resembled seaweed and did indeed cling to the rock like hair to a head. What had looked like an educational excursion on the school timetable was, Ant suspected, actually the use of his class as free slave labour.

"Careful chippin them there roots away; don't put a hole in your glove there, or it'll take root in your skin", cautioned the Sergeant. "It'll take root in steel iffen you give it a chance. We got to spray them concrete pillars yonder with pesticide an replace em once every five years."

He gestured at the support pillars for the perimeter fence, which did indeed look in a bad way. They were covered in plant life, and every time the wind blew, the one nearest to Ant creaked like his grandma's legs.

"How long since these pillars were replaced?" whispered Ant to Glenn Bob.

"About ten year", said Glenn Bob, looking up at the pillars in fear.

Ant looked up at the pillars, and down at the nearest rock pool to him, which was a beautiful, luminous blue.

He looked back at Glenn Bob. "You still ready to get out of here?"

Glenn Bob nodded.

Ant nodded back. "Then do exactly as I say. I have a plan which cannot fail."

***

They could still hear the screams of the school devegetating party behind them as they splashed through the freezing cold water of the rock pools.

"OW!" yelled Glenn Bob, as loudly as he could whilst still maintaining a whisper. "I got me bit for sure!"

"Rubbish!" said Ant. "It's just the cold of the water. They only *tell* you everything is venomous in order to keep you underground."

"Did we *have* to take off our boots?"

"Would Sergeant Sheldrake have believed we'd dived into a Nibbler leaving only our gloves?"

Glenn Bob shook his head dumbly.

"But only a pair of *complete lunatics* would run away after throwing their boots into a Nibbler stomach", said Ant proudly. "Therefore, the Sergeant will reason that the two pairs of boots and socks he found floating in that Nibbler back there are all that remains of our horribly mangled bodies."

"He might be right afore long", said Glenn Bob. "A kin't feel ma feet."

"Come on, it's only a hundred metres or so. How can we get stung or infected or otherwise killed inside a hundred metres?"

"Just you watch where you steppin", said Glenn Bob darkly.

***

Ant whispered into his communicator. "We're here."

"Where's here, idiot?"

"Airlock Thirteen."

"I thought we were going out of twelve!"

"There's been a change of plan. Airlock Thirteen is where the sickbay is."

There was a deep and brooding silence. Then: *"I've got to wheel this thing back past two supervisors."*

"Then you'd better hurry it up." Ant switched the communicator off. He realised that he was shivering. Glenn Bob, at his side, was doing likewise.

"A kin't feel ma feet", Glenn Bob repeated.

Ant switched the communicator on again. "Erm - and Cleo?"

"YES? What is it NOW?"

"Can you bring us a couple of changes of footwear?"

"And s-socks", said Glenn Bob.

"And socks", added Ant.

The communicator did not reply.

"I ain't goin nowhere without I wear socks", said Glenn Bob. "All them pictures of Huckleberry Finn wearin no socks was lies. Lies!" He looked at his corpse-white toes in great concern. "Tain't possible for a human bean to wear no socks for a protracted period of time in my opinion."

Ant turned his attention to the airlock. The lock was a huge, heavily corroded steel door sunk into the base of a cliff face. Ant remembered that the whole Croatoan colony was built into a flat-topped mesa - the airlocks might be the only way to get out and down to the land around it.

The lock had equally huge, rusted metal spikes poking out between the rocks around it, as if to protect anyone entering or leaving it against attacks by some gigantic creature.

"That's your Aboriginal Megafauna", said Glenn Bob, seeing Ant's amazement. "Sometimes they get through the wire."

There was no handle or knob on the outside of the airlock door - nothing but a depressingly large, corroded steel wheel, labelled MANUAL OVERRIDE. Ant remembered Sergeant Sheldrake's red face and bulging muscles as he'd worked the wheel on Airlock Twelve.

"You push up that side", he said to Glenn Bob. "I'll pull down on this one."

The wheel was a mass of rusted metal, and Ant was afraid of the steel breaking.

"PUSH!" he hissed.

"I AM PUSHIN", Glenn Bob hissed back.

The door also made a sound like a creaking door as soon as they leaned on it. But then, they both stumbled into the muck underfoot as the wheel suddenly turned a precious millimetre. They sat and let their breath come back, and then went at the wheel again.

Suddenly, a hideous gurgling cry rang through the air. Both boys stopped moving, and in Ant's case, breathing.

"What was that?" said Ant.

"Some sort of Megafauna, I imagine", said Glenn Bob. "Aboriginal too, shouldn't wonder."

He fell quiet a moment, then said:

"Usually they *don't* get through the wire."

The two of them threw themselves at the door like demons. It took what seemed like hours to turn the wheel all the way out of the metal, then a minute or so of hanging backwards off the door in very quiet panic to get the lock to open. Clumps of rust fell off it when it eventually did.

"We are *not* closing this door behind us", said Ant, and ran inside. The corridors stank like one long school changing room after the relatively fresh rotting weed smell of the outside, though the floors were noticeably cleaner than they had been a week ago. *Poor Cleo*, thought Ant. There were no signs for the sickbay. Glenn Bob explained that signs had been removed from most of Croatoan to hamper Communists if they ever invaded, and helpfully showed the way up a companionway to the floor above. Red alarm lights were blushing lethargically in the corridor roofs. "That's for us", said Glenn Bob. "We're Missing."

"We're not *very* missing", said Ant. "Not enough for them to waste any energy turning on a *proper* alarm system, at any rate."

Eventually, they came to a doorway cut into the rock of the corridor wall. A sign fixed above it, clearly legible by Communists, read SICKBAY, Y'HEAR.

The one bed inside was empty. A small note pinned to the pillow said:

YOU ARE TOO SLOW!!!!

I HAVE TAKEN MR. TURPIN. WILL RENDEZVOUS

WITH YOU AT THE REVISED RENDEZVOUS POINT.

C.

"Now there's efficiency", said Ant.

"What's a Rendezvuss?" said Glenn Bob.

"It's Spanish for rendezvous", said Ant.

"Gee willickers. Why didn't she just plumb say so."

"Let's get moving."

9 - Aboriginal Megafauna

When they got back to Airlock Thirteen, Cleo's beautiful clean floor was a mess. Not just one, but four pairs of feet seemed to have trailed dirt all over it. Two of the sets of footprints were small and bare, and were walking in from outside the colony. "That's us", said Ant. One set of prints was smaller still, wearing shoes with NIKE printed on the soles, and was going out, apparently pushing something that had wheels. "That's Cleo", said Ant.

The third set of prints had three toes and claws, and was going in.

"Erm", said Glenn Bob. "Maybe we should have shut that there door after ourselves after all."

"Cleo", said Ant in concern.

"No", said Glenn Bob, pointing to the tracks. "Her print is on top of the big one, see? It means she came out after it went in."

Ant stared at the huge clawprint. "Is that a Megafauna?"

Glenn Bob nodded with an air of knowledge. "Small one, of course", he added.

"More of a minifauna, then."

Glenn Bob seemed to come to a decision. He crossed the corridor, opened a panel in the wall, and pressed a button marked CAUTION USE ONLY IN EMERGENCY GOSH DANG IT. Alarms - far louder and more powerful alarms - began sounding.

Glenn Bob spoke into the wall. "This here is Glenn Bob Linklater speaking, y'hear. We have us a megafaunal intrusion situation at Airlock Thirteen. Small one about man size, no casualties as yet, fauna is headed in the direction of hydroponics."

Glenn Bob took his finger off the button. The alarms continued to sound. Ant stared at Glenn Bob open-mouthed.

"You've just told them we're alive, and where we are."

Glenn Bob stared at the wall defiantly. "Iffen that thing gets into the colony without warning, it will kill folks. *My* folks." As they walked back out into the sunlight, he swung the airlock door shut. "Help me dog this hatch." As Ant set to turning the wheel, Glenn Bob added: "Iffen we get caught now, pa'll stake me out in the swamps in pinchfly matin season with ma bewtocks smeared with molasses sure as dang an that's swearin."

As the door didn't need to be shut airtight, only megafauna-tight, they only needed to turn the wheel twice around; then they ran out, shivering in the cold air and water, and still being very careful where they put their feet.

"Well, *you* two couldn't make any more noise without a brass section and a PA system."

Cleo was standing on the deck of a rubber dinghy the size of a bouncy castle, floating in the middle of a rock pool which, Ant was relieved to note, was not beautifully blue. She was wearing rubber cleaning gloves, and had a Jackson's Deadly Carmine Sea Puff in the palm of one hand. "These little furry pink things are *so* cutesome. I keep wanting to just *kiss* them." She noticed Ant and Glenn Bob's expressions of alarm. "What? Is that bad?"

"How did you get back there without us?" said Ant.

"I came down the laundry lift", said Cleo, as if only fools didn't.

Mr. Turpin was lying in the dinghy, surrounded by a host of Carmine Sea Puffs. Glenn Bob scrambled gingerly onto the boat and knocked the things away from him with the back of his glove. Ant climbed aboard and inspected Mr. Turpin. He was still breathing.

Ant looked up at Cleo. Her own Carmine Sea Puff was attempting to climb up her arm past the end of her glove.

"Lose the fluffy pencil case, Cleo."

Cleo lost the Sea Puff. It splashed down into the water. When it tried to climb back out up onto the dinghy hull, Glenn Bob smacked it down again with the flat of his shovel.

"Did you bring the boots and socks?" said Ant urgently. Cleo nodded in the direction of a stack of crates in the opposite end of the dinghy, and Ant and Glenn Bob fell on them like starving vegetarians on a luckless radish.

"Ah, sweet, beautiful socks", sighed Glenn Bob.

"Which direction is Out Of Here?" said Ant.

Cleo shrugged. "I spent the last ten minutes inflating the boat." She brushed a Carmine Sea Puff off her shoe irritably.

Ant stared round the rock pool.

"Cleo", he said, "you've inflated it in a pool only a bit larger than it is."

Cleo followed Ant's eyes.

"Well", she said angrily, "you might concentrate on all the things I've done *right*, rather than niggling about one piffling little detail."

"Why did you think we needed a dinghy in the first place? You saw the land we came in over. There must have been at least a hundred miles of it."

"It might come in useful", said Cleo defensively.

"Very useful", nodded Glenn Bob vigorously in agreement.

"You hear that?" said Cleo. "*Bobby Glenn* thinks it's useful."

"I'm Glenn Bob", said Glenn Bob. "My brother's Bobby Glenn."

Ant leapt off the boat, narrowly avoiding capsizing it. Cleo and Glenn Bob swayed dangerously.

"Well", said Ant, "I'm going to make *myself* useful. We are going to have to get through this wire." He scrambled up to the nearest concrete pillar, which was overgrown with undevegetated weed, and launched a flying kick at it. The pillar swayed, but bounced back and nearly knocked Ant into the rock pool. All around Ant, the wires sang like harpstrings, but still sizzled with what sounded like a great deal of electricity.

"Ant", said Cleo severely, "what precisely are you trying to do?"

"This support pillar is the rottenest one in this section of wire, I reckon", said Ant. "Ever wonder why they wind these cables up so tight they scream in the breeze?"

"Nope", said Glenn Bob. "Iffen you miss that pillar base when you kick it, you gonna get yourself electrificated", he added helpfully.

Ant charged the base of the pillar again. This time, the pillar gave more than he'd been expecting, and he nearly sprawled forward onto the electrified wires. There were tiny PTANG-PTANG-PTANGs coming from the cables.

"Ant", said Cleo, "*please* stop doing that."

"They wind them up tight", Ant said, gulping for breath, "because most of the fence pillars are so badly eaten away that -" he charged the wire again - "they need the wires on either side to hold them up."

He collided with the fencepost. There was a terrific CRACK, a multiple TWANG, and a FZZZ-HSSSSS-PAZING. The fence collapsed around him like an electric octopus as all of its cables severed at once. Ant dived into the dirt, hugging the concrete pillar as it tumbled onto the rocks. Cleo and Glenn Bob ducked as the wires flailed overhead trailing sparks.

After a moment's pause, Ant sat back on his heels.

"Well", he said, "that's the fence down now."

"That was one of the most bizarre acts of stupidity I have ever seen", said Cleo.

Ant grinned. "There's a sort of rivulet over there. Shall we lift the boat and see if it fits into it?"

It took several minutes to heave the inflatable out of the water and over the dead cables without puncturing it on all the rock, concrete and steel. The boat slid gently into the small channel of water, which trickled down from a waterfall at the edge of the Croatoan mesa. Glancing upstream, Ant saw that steel bars had been fixed across the channel under the perimeter fence to stop anything from squirming into the colony by stealth.

"Let's go", he said.

Cleo handed out the oars, and Ant and Glenn Bob used them as best they could.

***

It became easier to paddle after a while; the oars stopped catching on the rocks, and the channel became wider. However, Ant felt that they were now paddling against a current.

"*Against the current?*", he said to nobody in particular, looking upstream to where the waterfall was still cascading down towards them.

His wrist communicator buzzed angrily. Automatically, he put it to his ear.

"*KIN YEW HERE ME THERE BOY*?" said the communicator.

Ant stared at the communicator without speaking. Glenn Bob and Cleo stopped pushing and paddling. The voice was shouting loudly enough for them to hear it too.

"*WE KNOW YOU DONE STOLE TWO RADIO TRANSCEIVERS. WE REQUIRE THEIR RETURN. YOUR IRRESPONSIBLE ACTIONS HAVE RESULTED IN THE DEATHS OF TWO CROATOAN CITIZENS.*"

Glenn Bob went whiter than a bleached sheet.

"They're lying", whispered Ant. "There's not been *time* for anyone to die."

"There's been time", said Glenn Bob, shaking his head. "Old man Goldspink got hisself gutted top to toe by a Megafauna in one go, and they only found the half of him."

"*IN VIEW OF YOUR TENDER AGES, WE ARE PREPARED TO COMMUTE CHARGES OF MURDER IFFEN YOU RETURN* IMMEDIATELY *AND SURRENDER ALL THE PROPERTY YOU DONE STOLE THERE, YOU GOT YOUR EARS ON?*"

"They'd never say so if we'd *really* killed anyone", said Cleo in a voice that suggested she was not entirely sure.

"*CERTAINLY*", the communicator gloated, "*THEM TRANSCEIVERS YOU DONE STOLEN ARE NOT CAPABLE OF COMMUNICATING WITH NO COMMUNIST VESSEL IN ORBIT. YOU WILL STARVE OUT THERE IN THE BARRENS BEFORE YOUR SOCIALIST ASSOCIATES ARRIVE TO PICK YOU UP. OVER.*"

"Ha!" said Ant. "Little do they know of our *other* transceiver in the ruins of Roanoke."

"Oh, they do", said Glenn Bob. "Whole dang town knows about *that*."

Cleo's jaw dropped. "Then that'll be the first place they'll LOOK!"

Glenn Bob appeared to consider this as if he hadn't before. "I reckon so", he conceded.

"*NOW HEAR THIS, GODLESS COMMUNISTS*", the wrist communicator buzzed. "*WE WILL SHORTLY BE CONDUCTING A THOROUGH SEARCH OF THE BARRENS AROUND OUR GREAT COLONY OF CROATOAN USING TRACKER GASTROPODS, AND WE* WILL *FIND YOU.*"

The rivulet seemed to be emptying out into a lake. Ant's paddle would not touch the bottom.

"Tracker *gastropods*?" said Ant.

Glenn Bob nodded. "Better'n dogs. A tracker slug can smell down a man over soil, sand, mud, even underwater. Iffen the feller climbs a wall to stop his scent going on the ground, the sluggie'll follow him plumb up the wall and across the ceiling. An if it gits him", said Glenn Bob with gruesome relish, "it eats out his eyes, an while he's still usin 'em too."

"You made up that last bit, didn't you", said Cleo.

"So what if I did", said Glenn Bob defensively. "The tracking part of it's true as Euclid's Fifth. My dad had him an old sluggie that sniffed out a thief two years after he'd done did the thievin, left the planet, travelled to sixteen different worlds and then come back again. And", Glenn Bob continued, as if this was even more amazing, "the feller'd had him at least one bath in that time too, with soap and all."

Cleo thought about this a second, then said: "So, basically your father was unable to catch the original criminal, so he picked on the first likely stranger to step off a ship and framed him."

Glenn Bob's eyes widened. "Aw no", he said. "My pa wouldn't do *that.*"

Ant stared down at the rivulet, which now seemed to have widened so much on either side that its banks could not be reached with his paddle.

"Hey", he said. "We're supposed to be fighting the current. How did we get so far downstream?"

Glenn Bob stared at him blankly.

"And furthermore", continued Ant, "why does downstream seem to be uphill?" He turned round to point upstream, in the direction of the waterfall, and gaped.

Upstream, the world had changed. The waterfall was still clearly visible, but was now tumbling off the edge, not of a mesa in the middle of a jumble of rocks and weeds, but of an island in the middle of a huge body of water that stretched from horizon to horizon.

"Where did the world go?" said Ant weakly.

"Tide's a-comin in", explained Glenn Bob.

"But we're a hundred miles inland", objected Ant.

"That's why it comes in so quick", said Glenn Bob. "We're as close to the coast as a Yankee is to a monkey."

"The tide comes *a hundred miles inland?*"

"Well, yeah", said Glenn Bob, in the same tone of voice Ant might have used to say, 'Well, yes, the horizon *is* usually found between the earth and the sky.' Ant then Ant remembered the dirty brown edges each continent on New Dixie had had when seen from space; bands hundreds of miles wide, like the soggy edges of a piece of tissue dropped on a wet floor.

"Three moons", he said. "You have three moons. And moons make tides."

"Can you smell that?" said Cleo.

Ant sniffed the air. If this was possible, there was actually something worse in it than the stench of rotting weed. Ant knew the smell from school science experiments. Mr. Postlethwaite had told them 'not to take in too much of a whiff from the test tube, or it'll sting like heck on legs'.

"Ammonia", he said.

Glenn Bob's face dropped.

"Aw, *no*", he said softly, staring into the sea underneath the dinghy's hull.

"What is it now?" said Cleo. "It's something bad again, isn't it."

"A Coldkraken", said Glenn Bob. "Mostly they live right down there on the sea bottoms, but sometimes young ones get fooled up into shallow water by cold water rising. They get big...*real* big..." He was now only whispering, staring down into the water in terror.

"How big?" said Cleo. "Or do I not really want to know?"

Ant pointed a trembling finger down into the water. Cleo followed the finger. In the depths under the dinghy, something big and round and silvery floated motionless.

"That's big enough", said Cleo.

"It's as big as the *boat*", said Ant.

"That", said Glenn Bob, "is its eye."

Ant sank back into the boat, very slowly. Glenn Bob continued to move his finger in the direction of Croatoan, to where the water seemed to change colour over the edge of a large sandbank. Then he drew the finger round in a circle till it pointed at the scarlet moon, which was setting. The sandbank extended all around them.

"That's not a sandbank, is it?" said Cleo.

Glenn Bob shook his head.

"We're plumb right above it. If we're quiet, it might let us alone and just think we're a lump of flotsam. But Coldkrakens usually live down in the deeps with their mouths open ready to eat what they can git. They'll eat just about any durn thing or body."

"Is there anything they *won't* eat?"

Glenn Bob thought a moment. "Um - rocks...avocado...certain types of steel..."

He appeared suddenly to have a brainstorm, picked up Cleo's paddle, and threw it overboard.

"GLENN BOB!" shouted Ant angrily.

"It's ornje", said Glenn Bob.

"What's an ornje?" said Cleo. "Don't tell me, it's probably something big and dangerous, probably venomous as well. I'm better off not knowing."

Glenn Bob looked confused. "An ornje", he said, "is a fruit. An also a colour", he added helpfully.

Ant looked down the front of his Croatoan uniform slowly. Like everything else in the landscape, it looked red.

He looked up at Glenn Bob helplessly.

"I give up", he said. "Is it ornje too?"

"It's ornje so as folk can find us iffen we get lost in the blizzards", nodded Glenn Bob.

"BLIZZARDS???" said Cleo.

"Ssssh", said Ant, pointing into the sea. "Remember who's downstairs."

Cleo looked down at her own uniform.

"Omigod", she said. "It's orange, it's orange, it's orange -"

"We know", said Ant and Glenn Bob together.

"Oh well", sighed Ant, looking at his new-found warm socks sadly, "I suppose there's nothing for it."

***

Ant, Glenn Bob and Cleo huddled together on the deck in a single huge American flag.

"I suppose we can only be thankful our pants weren't ornje as well", said Ant.

"Why would anyone put an American flag in a survival kit?" said Cleo.

"Iffen you spread it out, it makes you more visible from the air", said Glenn Bob. "An we had us a few thousand extra flags after we landed, pa said. Govermint wanted Roanoke Colony to have a population of five thousand by 1980, an every homestead was goin to have an American flag on its drive."

"On its drive", repeated Cleo. "Glenn Bob, you live in holes in the ground."

"I know", said Glenn Bob sadly. "Tell it to the megafauna."

"Shove over", said Ant. "I've only got the stars bit. You pair are hogging all the stripes."

Glenn Bob stared into the water. "Kraken's gone."

Croatoan Island was now only a black smudge on the horizon - the only black smudge in a sea of gently washing surf.

"Tide's come in real gentle today", said Glenn Bob. "Sometimes we gets breakers up to clifftop height."

Ant and Cleo stared at Glenn Bob venomously.

"I feel seasick", said Glenn Bob.

"Try swallowing ten times while holding your breath", said Ant.

"That's for hiccups", said Glenn Bob, "not seasickness."

"Try holding your breath and counting to a million, then", said Cleo nastily.

"I just wish the rocks on the horizon wouldn't keep *moving*", said Glenn Bob. Gamely, he began counting. "One - two - ah, three, there - ah, four -"

"ROCKS ON THE HORIZON", breathed Ant, as if this was somehow of great importance. Cleo stared at him oddly.

" - ah, five, six seven - eight, nine, ten -"

"You can't count *out loud*", snapped Cleo at Glenn Bob. "Every time you say something you breathe out!"

Ant shot to his feet. Cleo screamed. "ANT! YOU'LL CAPSIZE THE BOAT!"

Ant looked down at Cleo. The boat had not moved a millimetre. Cleo looked carefully at the horizon, then peered over the edge of the dinghy.

"Careful peering over the edge of the dinghy there", said Glenn Bob.

"Dry land!" shouted Cleo. "We're on dry land!"

There was, indeed, land under the dinghy - and it was getting drier. The jumble of rocks the boat had come to rest on was getting larger by the minute.

"Tide's going out", said Glenn Bob.

"Already?" said Ant.

"Moons move fast", said Glenn Bob. "We're goin to have to carry this here Inflatable. I still feel seasick", he added.

"*Carry* it? Why can't we leave it and walk?" said Cleo.

Glenn Bob spat with unerring accuracy at a passing Sea Puff. "Out here, a man always carries his Inflatable. Tide might in again in another few minutes. Maybe I'm *land*sick", he added.

Ant's wrist communicator hissed into life. "*NOW HEAR THIS, WE ARE ON YOUR TRAIL THERE COME BACK.*"

Ant did not Come Back, but instead struggled with Cleo and Glenn Bob to get the dinghy up onto their shoulders without dislodging Mr. Turpin, who was moaning softly.

"Why can't he wake up and pull his weight?" muttered Cleo. "Which is a great deal, incidentally."

"Where are we?" said Ant, looking up at the horizon, which now had considerably more than its previous share of small rocky islands.

"Cajuns' Column, at a guess", said Glenn Bob. "Cajuns' is the first spot in a mile to come up after a high tide. Excepting Croatoan, that is. And it's made of plutonic basalt, like these here rocks underfoot."

"You navigate by geology", said Ant.

"Got to. Landscape changes every half hour."

Mr. Turpin was just as heavy as Cleo had said. However, progress down from the top of Cajuns' Column would have been slow in any case, as the tide was only retreating at a slow walk.

"Couldn't we just put the dinghy down in the water and *float* downhill?" said Cleo.

"Not a chance", said Glenn Bob. "When the tide turns, you get out of the water quickeren stink, iffen you don't want to get yerself sucked in to the Roanoke Maelstrom."

"Maelstrom", said Ant.

"That'll go with the krakens and the blizzards and the Deadly Carmine Sea Puffs, then", said Cleo.

Glenn Bob nodded. "Only a mile off the shoreline. The maelstrom forms every high tide, travels back out to sea and breaks up again. It's a whirlpool a hundred miles wide. Cleans the seabed like a big old Electrolux."

Ant remembered the big spiral hurricanes he'd seen in the seas around the edges of New Dixie's continents from space. Suddenly, he realised they hadn't been hurricanes.

The communicator buzzed again.

"*WE HAVE PICKED UP YOUR VILE COMMUNIST SPOOR*", it said. "*OUR TRACKING GASTROPODS ARE CLOSE BEHIND YOU THERE, COME BACK.*"

Ant, Glenn Bob and Cleo looked around themselves in confusion. For miles in all directions, empty gurgling surf stretched out to the horizon.

"They's tellin lies", observed Glenn Bob darkly. "Don't you come back now, y'all."

"*WE CAN SEE YOU HIDIN THERE BEHIND THAT ROCK NOW*", insisted the communicator. "*GIVE YOURSELVES UP NOW THERE.*"

"Well, *they* obviously think they can see us", said Cleo.

A fainter noise could now be heard in the background on the communicator, yelling: "*Hold your fire there y'all! I ain't done nothin!*"

Glenn Bob yelped in delight. "That there's my twin brother, Bobby Glenn! Could be he smells just a little bit too like me."

The communicator rasped in triumph: "*NOW COME ON OUT THERE, VARMINT. HANDS ABOVE YOUR HEAD, DAGNABIT.*" A hideous sucking sound filled the speaker for a moment, and the same voice barked: "*DOWN THERE, SLUGGIE.*"

"We've got a head start", whispered Ant. "They'll take a while to realise they've got the wrong varmint."

"They'll pick up the trail again", promised Glenn Bob darkly. "A sluggie always gits his man."

"Then we'd better press on to Roanoke", said Ant. "Lift up your side there!"

Grunting and struggling, they heaved the dinghy onto their shoulders, and trudged downwards through a tumble of weed-grown boulders.

***

The sun Ant had once thought of as weak beat down pitilessly. All around, the drying weed was crackling with a sound like a steamroller driving over eggs. Ant was uncomfortably aware that, in nothing but boots and underpants, he was in danger of getting sunburn, and also looked amazingly stupid. Glenn Bob, in regulation Croatoan long underwear, would probably do better in the sunburn stakes, but certainly had picked the short straw in the stupidity ones. Cleo, meanwhile, appeared immune to the sun, and somehow managed to not look stupid at all. Ant reminded himself that this was because girls intrinsically looked better in underwear than boys.

"At least -" Ant puffed -" at least they can't hear us moving, with the weed making so much racket."

"They'll smell us out", moaned Glenn Bob. "There's sluggies on our tails right now, depend on it."

The dinghy, with Mr. Turpin in it, was impossibly heavy, and the weed underfoot hopelessly slippery. It was a wonder Mr. Turpin had not yet slipped off into a Nibbler and been Nibbled.

"We should be seeing this Roanoke place soon", gasped Cleo, "it's above sea level constantly, just like Croatoan, after all."

Glenn Bob frowned. "Not as such."

"WHAT?" Ant dropped his corner of dinghy, and narrowly missed dropping Mr. Turpin with it. "You mean Roanoke is UNDERWATER?"

"Not all of the time. Only at major conjunctions of the moons."

"So would you mind telling me how a radio transceiver can survive god knows how many years' immersion in salt water?"

"It might", said Glenn Bob defensively.

Ant let go of the dinghy altogether, forcing Glenn Bob and Cleo to put down their parts of it was well. Grumpily, he sat down next to Mr. Turpin's head. Mr. Turpin was drooling.

The wrist communicator buzzed again.

"WON'T TAKE US LONG TO PICK UP A FRESH TRAIL", it boasted. *"WE ARE ALSO ABOUT TO COMMANDEER US AN AERIAL SEARCH OF THIS HERE ENVIRONMENTAL VICINITY, AND YOU AIN'T GOIN NOWHERE. MR. GLENN BOB LINKLATER, YOUR POOR DEAR MOTHER URGES YOU TO COME BACK, COME BACK."*

"Let's face it", said Ant, "we're sunk. There's no way we can avoid being spotted from the air."

"BY COORDINATIN OUR EFFORTS BY AIR SEA AN LAND, WE SHALL BUILD AN EVER SHRINKIN BAG OF STEEL AROUND YOUR NECKS JUST LIKE RATS IN A MANACLE", said the communicator, and added: *"OUR TENTACLES ARE EVERYWHERE. Say, what's that overhead, Billy Hank?"*

"Don't know rightly. Looks like a big ole Cuban cigar. What's it look like on radar?"

"...uh...like God's clean air, Billy Hank."

"Only a Commie would build a ship that looks like a big ole Cuban cigar. HEY, YOU! GET OUT OF OUR SKY! THAT'S UNITED STATES OF AMERICA SKY!"

"BILLY HANK! DID YOU SEE THAT? IT DONE ZAPPED BILLY HANK -"

"IT'S HEADED FOR THE SETTLEMENT -"

"REGROUP, AND FOLLOW ME, SOLDIERS!"

"HEY, WHO ELECTED YOU LEADER THERE Y'ALL HSSSSSSSSSSSS -"

But Cleo didn't answer. She was busy staring at the horizon with wide eyes.

"The tide's coming in", she said.

"The tide's come in before", said Ant.

"No", she said. "I mean the tide's *really coming in.*"

Ant stood up and squinted into the sun.

"I see nothing", he said, "but a load of clouds on the horizon."

"Those aren't clouds", said Cleo. "They're wave tops."

10 - A Life On The Ocean Wave

"GOT IT", yelled Glenn Bob, meanwhile, wrapping the dinghy's mooring rope around a rocky outcrop, and then added: "THERE, Y'ALL!"

The dinghy was now bobbing in a narrow cove bombarded by freezing water. Every breaker threatened to throw the boat at the cliffs and burst it.

"WE GOT TO GET THE BOAT ASHORE", yelled Glenn Bob, "OR WE'LL ALL GET SUCKED BACK OUT INTO THAT THERE MAELSTROM WHEN THE TIDE TURNS, SURE AS YANKEES WEAR GIRLS' DRESSES."

Luckily, the tide still seemed to be driving into the rocks. They struggled the boat ashore, Glenn Bob and Cleo heaving on the mooring ropes from the shoreline whilst Ant ducked under the water to push the hull from underneath. Mr. Turpin smiled beatifically, and seemed to be attempting to eat the raindrops.

A distant gurgling sounded over the storm.

"NOT A JIFFY TOO SOON", bawled Glenn Bob. "THAT'S THE MAELSTROM FORMING UP THERE."

The wave fronts seemed to turn suddenly in the sea like an army changing facing to the right, and actual real solid boulders the size of cottages tumbled across the shoreline in the current, batted along like beachballs caught in a breeze.

"Tide's turnin", said Glenn Bob.

The wind began to die. Trees, rocks, and the occasional yowling megafauna sailed past, tumbling in the torrent. Ant shivered as he watched entire islets shiver from their moorings and roll into the bouncing surf. The entire horizon glugged like an emptying bathtub.

"That could have been us", he observed. Glenn Bob nodded gravely.

***

"Where *are* we?" said Ant.

Overhead, the sky was clearing, the storm apparently having travelled back out to sea with the tide.

Glenn Bob shrugged. "Don't rightly know", he said. "Tide like that could have pushed us inland clean off the map. Ain't no high ground with rock formations like this for a hundred mile around, excepting of course -"

He stopped dead, forcing Ant and Cleo to stop with him. Ant looked in the direction of Glenn Bob's gaze. There, leaning gently in two different directions, supporting strands of dripping high tension wire, were the unmistakeable shapes of two perimeter fence support pylons.

"- excepting back home", he said.

"Oh, *great*", said Cleo.

"Don't start", said Ant. "We can just lug the dinghy back down to the waterline, and -"

"And drown", said Cleo.

"Hold on there", said Glenn Bob. "There's smoke coming from that airlock there."

"How can there be smoke coming from an airlock", grumbled Cleo. "Airlocks can't catch fire."

But Glenn Bob had already dropped the dinghy's mooring rope and was running over the rocks towards the line of cliffs.

"Glenn Bob", yelled Cleo, "what in tarnation dagnabit are you doing?"

"Might be folk hurt", yelled Glenn Bob back.

Ant shrugged to Cleo, and they put down the dinghy, being careful not to tip Mr. Turpin, who was now growling like a dog and barking, and followed. The nearest airlock entrance was indeed belching smoke. As they approached it, they saw Glenn Bob picking around in the weed near the open lock door. Still wearing his devegetating gloves, he gleefully picked up a smoking cylinder which spat sparks, and waved it at Ant and Cleo as if picking up fizzing cylinders was clever.

"M99778234A(1) smoke round", he said. "Forty millimetre. Some folks was doing some close combat up here." He bent over and picked up a smaller, stubbier cylinder which looked half melted.

"What's that?" said Cleo.

Glenn Bob looked at the thing he'd picked up in the same way Ant might have looked at a sloughed king cobra skin he'd found in his bed.

"M84322497A1B1 armour piercing round", he said. "Forty millimetre. It...*bounced off* something." He bent down to the corridor floor and picked up something else. "Oh, and lookee here - this here is the piece they done fired it out of. M84322497A heavy rocket grenade launcher."

"So if someone was shooting at something with it", said Cleo, "where are they now?"

"No Croatoan citizen", said Glenn Bob, "leaves his piece behind." He thought a moment, and then added: "No live citizen, anyhow." He said nothing more.

Ant ran a finger along the corridor wall. Instead of the usual layer of filth, a greasy residue came off on his fingertips.

"Gosh", he said. "Don't they ever clean in here?" Cleo looked at him severely.

"Looks like oil", said Glenn Bob.

"Feels like warm Swarfega -" Ant said, then added "OW!" and rubbed his hands together to rid himself of the goo. "*OW!*" he continued, and attempted to pull his hands apart again without success. He held them up to his face. A thin layer of blue goop, the colour visible in the electric light from the doorway, was creeping over his hands towards his wrists.

"JEEZ", he said, and then, turning to Glenn Bob and Cleo, "get it off! Get if off!"

After many long moments of awed staring, Glenn Bob was suddenly galvanized into action. Unfortunately, this action amounted to trying to rub the goop off Ant's hands using his own. "I DONE STUCK MYSELF!" he yelled. His other hand went into his pocket and came out holding a claspknife. "GUESS THE ONLY ANSWER'S AMPYTATION AFORE IT GITS TO OUR BRAINS!"

"IT'S ALREADY GOT TO YOURS", yelled Ant. The circle of goop had now reached his wrists, and he could feel it moving up towards his elbows.

"I GOT TO DO YOUR HANDS FIRST AFORE I DO MINE", yelled Glenn Bob, "OR I MIGHT PASS OUT WITH THE PAIN. HOLD STILL THERE, DAMN AND DANG YOU." The two struggled backwards and forwards across the corridor, Glenn Bob attempting to dig his claspknife into Ant's infected arms. Meanwhile, Cleo seemed to have vanished. The goop glove had now reached Ant's elbows.

Suddenly, Cleo returned bearing an armful of plastic bottles. "Cleaning solvents", she announced, before popping the top off a bottle and rapidly pouring something over Ant's arm that felt like a mouthful of nettles. Ant yelped in pain.

"I'M GUESSIN I'LL HAVE TO TAKE THE WHOLE ARM THERE NOW", screamed Glenn Bob. The goop envelope was rising toward Ant's armpit, and showed little sign of stopping.

"Aha, no response from bleach", said Cleo, the analytical chemist. "Let's try ammonia." Ant's arm burned again, and he shrank away from Cleo's sponge as she dabbed a second horrid substance on it. The goo membrane crawled up onto his shoulder, and even seemed to glow a healthier shade of green as it drank up whatever Cleo had soaked it with.

"It's moving toward my mouth", said Ant in panic, pushing Glenn Bob away.

"Don't worry", said Cleo, "I've still got hydrochloric acid in reserve." She dabbed a milky white substance onto Ant. Ant hoped it wasn't hydrochloric acid. It looked enough like Brasso for Ant to imagine it might not burn. It burned. However, at its touch, the goop thing covering his arm, chest and neck crisped, crackled and fell away.

"That was effective", breathed Ant. "What was it?"

"Something called Drano", shrugged Cleo. "I never used it. Could be vegan mayonnaise for all I know."

"I think it's safe to assume", said Ant, wiping his red raw arm clean with rock pool water outside the airlock entrance, "that it isn't mayonnaise."

Glenn Bob sat against a boulder, scraping his arm clean on the boulder's coating of extraterrestrial space barnacles. He carried on scraping until his arm bled.

"Whatever that blue goo is", said Ant, "I think it's fair to say it's what did for the Croatoan colonists at this airlock."

"If not all the colonists", said Cleo. "We haven't heard from any of them on the communicator for hours."

"Well, yes", said Ant. "But that's just because the communicator's not work -"

He stared down at his communicator. He raised it to his lips and said, slowly and carefully, "Testing, testing, testing. One, two, three."

Sure enough, he could hear his own tiny tinny voice coming from the communicator still wrapped around Cleo's wrist. Glenn Bob looked as if he were about to cry.

Suddenly, something cold and clammy brushed against Ant's leg. Ant jumped.

***

"What *is* it?" said Ant, as the cold clammy thing slithered around his ankles like a very slow cat.

"Why, that's our champion slitherin sleuth, Truman J. Slughound III", said Glenn Bob delightedly, dropping to his knees and slapping them. "Someone done survived, then, didn'tcha there, boy? Here, boy!"

"I thought he was going to eat my eyes", said Ant mistrustfully.

"Nah", said Glenn Bob. "Old Slughound here has twenty nine thousand teeth, but they're all fer eatin weed."

Truman J. Slughound resembled nothing so much, as his name suggested, as a metre-long slug with far too many eyestalks. He was also disconcertingly changing colour in flickers of electric blue and green.

"He's a Sluggie", said Cleo.

"Diggety-danged right", said Glenn Bob. "Best tracking sluggie in the whole of New Dixie. He's bin set to track you down, and now he's pleased he's found you." He looked round himself in puzzlement. "Don't see no sign of no Sergeant Sheldrake in hot pursuit, mind."

"Sergeant Sheldrake", said Cleo, "is dead. He was eaten by that", she pointed in the direction of the tunnel, "that, that *goo*."

The sluggie curled up around Ant's ankles and retracted its eyestalks contentedly.

"That's means he's goin to sleep", said Glenn Bob.

"How long for?" said Ant. With the sluggie wound around him, it was surprisingly difficult to move.

"Normally the entire winter", said Glenn Bob. "Mind, he's domestycated there, so -"

Glenn Bob was interrupted by a colossal rumble from the sky. He stared up in disbelief.

"GET DOWN!" he yelled. "SOME COMMIE YANKEE SON OF A DEVIANT IS LANDING A SAUCER ON FULL DRIVE!"

The rumble shook through the rocks underfoot and made the weed that clung to them vibrate. Glenn Bob dived behind a boulder. Ant had to bend to pick up the sluggie coiled around his feet before he could begin to move. Truman J. Slughound felt, if anything, even slimier than he looked, and pulsed orange and red in annoyance as Ant uncurled him from his ankles. Ant dived into cover behind Glenn Bob and Cleo.

"Why is it so dangerous to be close to a saucer landing on full drive?" said Cleo.

Glenn Bob pointed. "Watch the weed", he said. "*Watch the weed.*"

Sure enough, the Gorgons' Hair all over the boulderfield nearby was crumpling, dying and dissolving, curling in on itself, turning from a living brown carpet into dust as if an invisible wave of death were sweeping through it. The wave swept up towards the boulder where Ant, Cleo and Glenn Bob were hiding. Truman J. Slughound made an attempt to ooze up into Ant's lap. Glenn Bob slapped it away irritably.

"Bad sluggie!" said Glenn Bob. "Bad sluggie, there! Sluggies ain't allowed on laps nor beds nor shoulders!"

Then, miraculously, before it could reach their boulder, the wave of destruction stopped.

"They done turned off their motor", said Glenn Bob. "Whoever it is, they done landed."

"They might be friendly", said Cleo.

"Only the military land on full power", said Glenn Bob. "And they only do it in combat zones."

"They're probably the same lot who gooped the colonists", said Ant pessimistically, "coming back for us."

"No", said Cleo suddenly, shaking her head firmly. "Absolutely not."

Ant frowned at Cleo. "Explain", he said.

"Well", said Cleo, "why would they have got into a gunfight down here with the Croatoan people when they could have just killed everyone with a full power landing?" Her face took on an expression of intense concentration, as if she was only just now working out what she was saying. "Whoever was here before, whoever spread the goop, didn't come to kill. They came to capture."

"So my mom and dad might still be alive someplace", said Glenn Bob hopefully.

Cleo thought this over, and nodded grudgingly.

"Great", said Ant. "So by your own logic, whoever's just landed now doesn't care whether or not they kill us."

Cleo frowned and nodded. "I'm afraid so."

***

The sound of voices could be heard. The voices were shouting, but Ant could not understand what was being said. At first he thought this was because the voices were so far away. As the voices came steadily closer, however, he began to realise that this was because they were not shouting in English.

"Why's it taking so long for them to get to us?" said Cleo.

"They landed on top of the mesa", said Glenn Bob. "They got the whole of the Croatoan tunnels to get through between themselves and us."

Eventually, however, the shouting became accompanied by footsteps, coming closer. Peering round the edges of the boulder up the airlock tunnel, Ant saw a group of green-uniformed figures carrying guns, moving rapidly in formation, each one covering the other as he moved.

"I don't know who they are", said Ant to Cleo, "but they could be our ticket out of here."

"Are you CRAZY?" hissed Glenn Bob. "They're COMMIES."

"Glenn Bob", said Ant, "I know this is hard for you to believe, but Commies don't really exist any more since about, oh, the mid nineteen eighties, except in North Korea and parts of Camden."

"LOOK AT THEIR UNIFORMS, gosh darn it!"

Ant looked at the uniforms. Each one had a huge red star on the shoulder. Granted, there was a spaceship going round the star, but it was a star nevertheless, and it was red. And the non-English language that the men were shouting to each other did indeed sound remarkably like Russian.

However, one of the soldiers was about to put his hand on a Jackson's Carmine Sea Puff.

Ant ransacked his memory for the only few words of Russian he knew. He shot to his feet.

"NIET!" he yelled, pointing to the Sea Puff. "NIET NIET NIET!"

Three rifle barrels turned unerringly in Ant's direction. Ant raised his hands very, very slowly. The soldier still had his hand poised over the Puff. "NIET NIET!" yelled Ant, pointing at the thing with both hands above his head and managing to look surprisingly like a rap artist as he did so. This time, one of the Russians seemed to understand, and barked something at the would-be Puff-fondler, who looked down at the beast with an expression of bored distaste and removed his hand.

The Russian who had barked the order bawled something rapid and unintelligible at Ant. Ant attempted to shrug without putting his hands down. "Englishski?" he said.

"Angliskii?" said the soldier in charge.

"Er - da", replied Ant.

The officer nodded, and beckoned to Ant. Still with his hands up, Ant moved in the man's direction. The rifles on either side of Ant followed him as he walked until the officer screamed at his men again and they lowered their weapons sheepishly. The officer shrieked back into the airlock as if summoning someone else. Then he peered inquisitively at the boulder Ant had jumped up from behind.

"You may as well come out", said Ant. "I think he knows you're there."

11 - Red Star Rising

The Russian ship was saucer-shaped, which Ant was by now prepared for. It was also covered in red stars, hammers and sickles, which was more surprising.

"I thought the Russians got bored with all this sort of stuff years ago", said Ant.

"*I* thought the Americans had banned slavery", said Cleo crossly.

If the American corvette *Virginia* had been a flying dinnerplate to Mr. Turpin's saucer, this new ship was a veritable soup tureen. It was so large, it seemed more like a fixed, permanent structure, like an oil rig or a gasometer, than something that was capable of moving through the air under its own power. There were details on it that Ant knew must be the as big as he was, but which were too faint and far away for him to be able to see them clearly. It also bristled with things that were almost certainly weapons. Every available inch of it had been painted a deep green that identified it to any observer as a military ship. And it was plastered with as many deep red stars as a bloodstained galaxy.

The ship was surrounded by a splat of blasted earth, no doubt because it had just landed on full power. The landing also appeared to have melted all of the Croatoan spaceport dish antennas on one side, making the steel run like treacle. A point at the bow of the vessel had dropped open like a colossal jaw, and small caterpillar-tracked vehicles were trundling up and down this ramp. Some of the vehicles held what looked like scientific equipment, and at least one of them was clearing the muck from around the ship's massive landing legs with a small dozer blade, but the vast majority of them were actually travelling up the ramp laden with goods taken from inside Croatoan.

Glenn Bob was incensed. "HEY!" he yelled. "HEY STOP THIEF!" Ant recognised a photograph of Glenn Bob's brother on one of the caterpillar trucks, along with a set of wooden chairs and tables that could only have come from Earth. On Croatoan, he knew, such stuff would be very valuable.

"WHERE YOU TAKIN THAT!" bawled Glenn Bob. "THAT'S MY MOM'S!" He tried to rush the Russian trooper driving the truck, but was pushed back by a sentry. Three times he tried to get close to the truck, and three times he was pushed back. The other Russian soldiers appeared to find Glenn Bob's battle with the sentry amusing, and stopped their work to watch, until finally the man pushed Glenn Bob so hard he fell back into the dirt and turned a rifle on him. Glenn Bob stared at the rifle barrel in disbelief, but did not try again.

An officer - Ant decided he must be an officer because of his cap and shoulderflashes - saluted Ant and Cleo. Ant saluted back. The officer laughed and bent down to Ant's level like a kindly uncle. Ant, who had been brought up to strongly distrust strangers who tried to behave like kindly uncles, did not let his guard down one iota. One of the tracked vehicles going into the saucer, he noticed, now had Mr. Turpin in it, gurgling happily like a baby.

"Where are you taking him?" said Ant. "He is ill. He is being treated for a bullet wound."

"He will be very good very soon", said the kindly officer. "Be welcome to our shyip, small comrades. I am Cyaptain Igor Popov of the First Red Star Armada." He gestured up at the enormous dull green saucer, which stretched over their heads like the dome of an upturned cathedral. "Is our shyip, the *Alexei Stakhanov*."

"This", said Glenn Bob, picking himself up off the floor defiantly, "is a Act of War."

"*Glenn Bob*", said Ant through the corner of his mouth, "*why are there Russians in space?*"

Glenn Bob hissed back through gritted teeth. "*Commie traitors sold em the blueprints for the Astromoke Mark One back in '53. They bin in space ever since.*"

"*And they're communists?*"

"*Sure. They're Russkies. Ain't all Russkies commies?*"

"*Not on Earth any more, no.*"

Glenn Bob was struck dumb by this unexpected news. Captain Igor Popov, meanwhile, was more talkative.

"Is not an act of war please", he said. "Is replying to a Myayday Call. There was Yinternational Myayday Call from this location."

"We wouldn't make no Mayday Call to no Russkie", said Glenn Bob.

"Aha!" pounced Captain Popov. "Thyen logically, you *would* make a Myayday Call to a Russkie. Is Yinglish Double Nyegative, no?"

"I hate people who point that out", muttered Ant to Cleo.

"We nyeed to know please why is no pyeople here."

"Stop saying everything with a 'y' in it", said Cleo.

"I'm nyot", said Captain Popov, wounded. "Why is no pyeople here?"

"We don't know", said Ant.

"Maybe pyeople here have offyended evil American capitalist gyovernment. Maybe they have been tyaken away, put in labour camp."

"*Put* in a labour camp?" said Cleo in disbelief. "This *is* a labour camp." Noticing Glenn Bob's laserbeam stare, she retorted: "Well it was for *me*. *You* didn't have to do any *washing*."

"As I suspyected", said Captain Popov. "Do not worry. You are now in hyands of Byeautiful Socialist Utopia. Captain of ship, Lieutenant Gushin, shall I think order we do the take-off very soon." He made illustrative spaceship-taking-off gestures with his hands. "To come with me, please."

"*Captain* of the ship? And he's only a Lieutenant? If you're a Captain", accused Cleo, "why aren't you the Captain, Captain?"

Captain Popov smiled broadly. His teeth were in a terrible state. "Ah, but I am not Nyaval Officer, I am only KGB."

"This", said Ant, "goes from bad to worse."

***

"Please not to worry please. We are only asking questions. All we require is answers."

The room was grey and featureless. All it contained was a desk, four chairs, and a door, all made of the same grey steel as the walls, floor and ceiling. Even the light, coming from a strip bulb overhead, was grey.

Ant, Glenn Bob, and Cleo were sitting on one side of the desk. Captain Popov was sitting on the other. Behind Captain Popov - presumably in case the three thirteen-year-olds in the room overpowered him - stood a uniformed Russian soldier with a gun. The gun appeared to be a Russian version of the ones British and American space people used. Ant had no doubt that it would kill him.

At the moment, however, it was Captain Popov who was being interrogated.

"YOU DONE SMOKED EVERYBODY IN MY COLONY", raged Glenn Bob with tears of anger in his eyes.

"He's going to get us sent to some sort of Astro Siberia", Cleo warned Ant quietly.

"Oh, I think he's getting calmer", whispered Ant. "He hasn't called the Captain a hornswoggling varmint son of a jackalope for at least five minutes now."

Captain Popov shook his head slowly.

"Glorious Soviet Yutopia does not kyill wyomen and chyildren", he said, and appeared to believe what he was saying.

"So you're asking us to believe that your ship just *happened* to turn up here only a few hours after Croatoan was wiped out", said Ant.

"You will plyease explain also why Yunited States of Zodiac myilitary pilot is here", said the Captain. "Is Yunited States of Zodiac shyip here also. Astromoke Mark One."

"He's talking about Mr. Turpin's ship", said Cleo.

"So Mr. Turpin *is* from the USZ", said Ant.

"Ha!" Captain Popov's face was triumphant. "As I suspyected! So Yunited States of Zodiac *is* respyonsible for extyerminating innocent Amyerican citizens of Croatoan."

"I didn't say that", said Ant.

"You dyid", said Captain Popov, raising an accusing finger against Ant.

"No, *you* did", said Glenn Bob, "you slug-chugging crawdad spawn."

The Captain slammed his hand down on the table. "You will tell us sordid truth of fighting between Amyerican Yimperialist factions. We know truth alryeady. All is nyeeded is confirmation. You will also tyell us plyease location of Yunited States of Zodiac Syecret Gondolin Colony and syecret Yamerican yingredient of Coca-Cola."

"I'll tell you I'm Glenn Bob Linklater, Citizen Number 1233", said Glenn Bob, "and diddly squat more."

The Captain stared darkly across the table.

"Yunited States of Zodiac trooper will give us answers", he said. "Will give us *considerably* more than Sqvat." He glared from Glenn Bob to Ant to Cleo. "Is your father, this man, perhaps? Your brother?"

"So you're threatening to torture Mr. Turpin", said Ant.

"You, sir", said Glenn Bob, "are a godless Commie fiend."

"You thought Mr. Turpin was one an hour ago", said Cleo.

Glenn Bob, evidently confused, shut up.

"You will admyit colony of New Dixieland was attacked by United Styates of Zodiac", said the Captain, "or you will be responsible for your Myister Turpin."

"Don't do it, Glenn Bob", said Ant. "How many planets in the United States of the Zodiac?"

"'bout twelve", said Glenn Bob.

"With how many people on them?"

"Dunno", said Glenn Bob. "Hundreds. Could be thousands, even."

"And how many people live in the United States' colonies in space?"

"Thousands", said Glenn Bob. "Tens of thousands."

"And what would happen if the US colonies thought the USZ had attacked one of their outposts and killed everyone in it?"

Glenn Bob thought a moment.

"War, I guess", he said. "Though we're at war with the US Zee already there", he added quickly. "But right now it's that sort of war folks don't get killed in."

"And if those two nations go to war", said Ant, "tens of thousands of people might die. American fighting American."

"But they might *kill* Mr. Turpin", said Cleo.

Ant nodded. "Better one man than a thousand", he said. "And he *did* kidnap us."

The Captain pointed his finger at Ant again. This time, it was shaking.

"You will tell truth", he said, rose from the table, and stalked out.

Ant and Cleo exchanged frowns.

Then, the trooper by the door bent over and whispered in Cleo's ear.

"You should tyell truth", he said. "Is byest for all of us."

Cleo stared at the soldier in disbelief. "You speak English too!" she said.

The soldier waved his hands frantically at her to be quiet, staring after his departing captain. "I have learned beautiful Yinglish language from lyistening to transmyissions from Earth", he said conspiratorially. "At my home on Altair 5 I watch all Yinglish television. I like very much your Amyerican Banana Splyits. Mister Drooper taking out trash, ha! ha! is most amusing."

Cleo stared at the trooper blankly.

"Altair is thirty light years from Earth", said Glenn Bob. "It takes radio waves thirty years to get there. He's talking about some show from 1969, I reckon."

"Is correct!" beamed the trooper. "You dumb Amyericans only just land on moon, ha! ha!"

"We done landed on the moon in 1951", said Glenn Bob. "There's a third man in they there 1969 moon pictures, and don't you fergit it."

The trooper shook his head. "Russians land on moon first after applying secrets of alien science found yin Yextraterrestrial Flying Saucer that is exploding in Tunguska in 1908. Amyericans stole this secret from Mother Russia. Every Russian schyoolboy knows this."

Glenn Bob stared at the trooper, slack-jawed at the man's audacity.

"I wonder who's right", grinned Ant, "the Americans or the Russians?"

"Where's this secret Gondolin colony?" said Cleo.

"Gondolin's the thirteenth colony of the United States of the Zodiac", said Glenn Bob wearily. "No-one knows where it is, exceptin the Zodiackers. Course, these jokers think you do too, on account of they think you're Zodiackers. If y'all *do* know where it is, I strongly suggest spillin your guts", he looked up at the trooper sourly, "before they do."

"I must gyo now", said the trooper. "'Size of an Yelephant!' Ha! Ha! Ha!"

He stepped outside the cell and pressed a button. Two steel doors a man's arm thick clanged into place over the doorway just as alarms sounded, voices yelled over the intercom in Russian, and the deck under Ant and Cleo's feet began rumbling for takeoff. In the centre of the doors, a piece of glass thick enough to bend light like water showed the trooper's smiling face waving goodbye for now.

***

"Well", said Cleo, "that went well, I thought."

"I ain't never gonna to see my maw and paw again", blubbed Glenn Bob.

"Now you know how we feel", said Ant.

"I thought you were running away from your maw and paw?" said Cleo.

"Not *really*", said Glenn Bob. "I was just attention-seekin."

"Well, you've got our attention now", said Cleo. "So how are we going to get out of here?"

"In a box, I reckon", said Glenn Bob.

Ant, meanwhile, was standing on tiptoe, looking out of the cell's only window.

"What can you see?" said Cleo.

"A sort of guardroom-cum-office-cum-wardrobe", said Ant. "Captain Popov is sitting at a workstation in one corner. His desk is very messy. All the other consoles in the room are piled high with all the swag they nicked from Croatoan. There's three blokes in there going through it all. One man's wearing a lampshade on his head. Another man seems to have found a pair of outsize red and white polka dot ladies' undies, and appears to find this riotously amusing."

Glenn Bob's face scrunched up into a snarl. "Them's my mom's!" he growled.

"Well, there's a big fat soldier wearing them now. The others are joining in the general hilarity. A third man seems to be trying to shave with a jar of marshmallow fluff, with surprising success."

"That there fluff is US Colony of Croatoan property."

"Well, I wouldn't be too bothered, they're ignoring most of the Croatoan stuff. They seem to be more interested in what Mr. Turpin was smuggling in his saucer. Particularly the whisky." His eyes went wide as he gawped through the door. "No. Surely it isn't possible for a human being to drink whisky that fast, not without - ah, yes, he's vomiting now."

"Aha!" said Cleo. "We wait till all the guards are drunk, and - and -"

"- and burrow through the solid steel of the door", said Ant.

"Well, if you're so clever, *you* think of something", said Cleo, and sat back on the chair with her arms folded.

Then, abruptly, she fell flat on the floor.

"OW!" she yelled. "That' not FUNNY, Glenn Bob!"

"I didn't do nothin", protested Glenn Bob.

"YOU PULLED MY CHAIR AWAY -", she shouted, pointing at her chair - then, gawping in disbelief, said:

"Where's my chair?"

The chair, along with the other three chairs and the table, had disappeared into the grey steel of the floor, becoming flush with it.

The metal of the walls began to creak and tick, as if someone, somewhere, had turned on the central heating.

"Hey!" yelled Glenn Bob, leaping back from the cell wall. "This wall's gone colderen a snowman's icehole!"

"He's right", said Ant, touching the steel. "It's freezing."

"This is a purpose-built interrogation cell", said Cleo. "They can probably alter the temperature to make prisoners more or less comfortable."

"The air's getting colder", said Ant.

"Then we'd better give them the story they want, or we'll freeze", said Cleo. As she spoke, air intakes howled open in the walls. It felt as if all the warmth were being sucked out of the room via a huge vacuum cleaner.

"OK. OK, let's confess", said Ant, realising his teeth were beginning to chatter.

"Of course, you realise that as soon as we do that, they're bound to shoot Mr. Turpin", said Cleo the inexorable logician.

"Th-they will?" said Ant. "But th-they said they'd s-stop interrogating him once we told the t-truth."

"That's p-perfectly true", said Cleo. "Th-they'll stop interrogating him, and sh-shoot him instead. Once they have our c-confession, they d-don't need to b-beat one out of him any more, do they?"

"Then we don't confess", said Glenn Bob. Ant and Cleo turned to look at him. Glenn Bob wore an expression of determination so fierce it hurt to look at him.

"I'm d-danged if I'm giving up any m-man to any d-darned Commie", he said. "Even if he *is* another C-commie", he added, and a little bit of doubt seemed to creep into his determined expression, but he set his teeth and scowled until it went away.

"Then I suggest", said Ant, "that we huddle together for warmth. Keeping, of course," he said, catching Cleo's hostile glance, "a respectable distance at all times."

12 - Show and Tell

"You will explain please", said the Captain, "purpose of device."

Ant and Cleo stared across the table at the device. The warmth was only beginning to creep back into their toes and fingers. It was quite obvious that the temperature had only been turned up for the Captain's comfort, and that as soon as he left the room and the interrogation was over, the air would turn frosty once again; but this did not alter the fact that the temporary warmth felt good.

The device stared back at Ant and Cleo across the table. The Captain had woken it up by shouting, and it had opened its enormous plastic eyes.

The Captain clapped his hands twice quickly. The device flapped its ears enthusiastically. "Hey kah ay-ay u-nye", said the device.

"Hyas done this many tyimes now", said Captain Popov. "My syoldiers are alarmed."

"It's a Furby", said Cleo.

"Fyur-bee", repeated the Captain.

"You can speak to it in Furbish", said Cleo.

"Fyur-byish", said the Captain. "You will please state device's plyanet of origin."

"It's an alien", said Ant. Cleo gave him a dig in the ribs. "Why not?" he said to Cleo. "Why not tell the truth, I mean. It's a sentient life form from, erm, the galaxy of Arcturus."

"Is no intelligent life in space", said the Captain.

"Well, you're certainly proof of that", muttered Cleo in a low voice.

"Also", said the Captain, "device does not move. Cyannot be alive."

"It is telepathic", said Ant. "It does not need to move."

"Is device", pooh-poohed the Captain. "Is yartificial thying. Has switch on bottom."

"The visible portion of the Furby", explained Ant, warming to his subject, "is a highly sophisticated life support system, containing the actual organism deep inside. The life support system has eyes and ears and feet only in order not to alarm races less telepathically gifted than itself. Its powers of the mind are all-reaching. It can Read Your Inmost Thoughts."

The Captain looked at the Furby in dread. Then, he seemed to recover slightly, and asked: "If yis very powerful, why yis still my pryisoner?"

"It's probably judging your fitness to join the Galactic Federation or something", said Ant - and then, in a moment of brilliance, added: "the Galactic *Communist* Federation."

Captain Popov's eyes bulged out of his head. Then an expression of crafty distrust crept across his face.

Looking at Ant, he raised his voice and said: "Comrade Fyurby."

"Doo-moh may-lah kah", said the Furby.

"What is Yimmediate aim of World Communism?"

"Dah lee-koo wah", said the Furby.

"Ha! Complyetely wrong", said the Captain. "Answer is formyation of proletariat into class and overthrow of bourgeois supremyacy."

"He *did* say the answer", protested Cleo. "He just said it in Furbish!"

"Enough!" said the Captain, and pounded on the table hard enough to send the Furby bouncing. "Cyonical thying is not Yalien. Yis no yintelligent yalien life yin spyace." He squinted at the Furby like a gunfighter staring down an opponent.

"Is myade of plyastic", he said victoriously, as though only an extremely detailed observation could have revealed this.

"Hey kah mee-mee ay-tay wah!", said the Furby.

"There are animals on New Dixie that *eat* plastic", said Ant.

"Ha!" said the Captain. "Then we styake Fyurby out on New Dixie syurface. It will soon talk and tell us whyether is Yalien or not." Triumphantly, he rose from the table and walked out, hands clasped behind him.

"Haha!" echoed the guard. "One byanana two byanana three byanana four, is very funny! Ha! Ha! Ha!"

He pressed the button to close the door, and all sound from the outside world was cut off.

***

"He's made a mistake", said Ant, squinting through the door glass at the Captain sitting down at his desk.

"How so?" said Cleo.

"He left something behind."

"Gosh", said Cleo, hugely unimpressed. "What can it be? A tungsten carbide drill, perhaps? A Get Out Of Cell Free card? Maybe some sort of magic wand that only Ant can see?"

Ant, however, was beaming at the Furby with a glint of insane confidence in his eyes.

"Every time", said Ant, "that Captain Popov comes into this cell, he uses no key, keypad or keycard of any kind. Instead, he says something once into a point on the wall next to the door. The *carefully soundproofed* door. I", he added with vast superiority, "have been *watching*, while certain people have been just been shivering in the corner and *complaining.*"

"I see the beginnings", said Cleo, "of a plan even more moronic than is usually your wont."

"You speak Furbish, don't you", said Ant.

"Like a native", said Cleo. "I have three little sisters, none of whom can be bothered to read the user manual for the damned things."

Ant sat down and peered closely into the Furby's eyes. "Comrade Furby", he said, "you are about to carry out a mission vital to the security of the civilized world. Are you up to it?"

"Kah ay-ay e-tah", said the Furby.

***

"You will please report progress in re-yeducation of allyeged cyonical Yalien", said the Captain.

"We have managed, we believe", said Cleo, "to get through a number of basic English phrases to the Furby."

The Captain narrowed his eyes at the tiny creature. "Procyeed", he said.

Cleo bent to the Furby's level, and said, loudly and clearly in its ear, "Hey u-nye lee-koo".

"All Power to the Soviets", said the Furby. "Peace, bread, freedom."

The Captain sat back in his chair, and fiddled with his glasses.

Then, he began to scowl again.

"Yis speaking Yinglish. Is not speaking Russian. You make it speak Russian please."

"Sadly", said Cleo, "I cannot teach the Furby Russian, as I do not myself speak it."

The Captain banged the table with his fist again, making both Cleo and the Furby jump. "*Is tyelepathic!* Can spyeak any lyanguage!"

Ant put up his hand. "Please, sir - it's only *one-way* telepathy. The Furby can understand anything you say, but can only reply in Furbish."

The Captain nodded, absorbing this.

Then, he thumped his chest, and announced:

"I will remove Fyurbish Yalien to syeparate confinement. *I* shyall teach Russian to Yalien, using Superior Soviet Yintelligence."

He picked up the Furby, cradled it as if he were jealous of Cleo's influence over it, and cooed to it in Soviet.

Then, suddenly remembering himself, he pointed a finger at Ant, Cleo and Glenn Bob.

"You wyill tell truth", he said, rose from the table, and stole out cooing to his Furby.

"Snyorky!" said the guard. "Honk honk honk honk honk!" and left.

The doors slid closed, deadening all sound from the outside world.

A big grin spread across Ant's face.

"It begins", he said.

Then, a joyful whoop from Glenn Bob clanged off the cell walls.

"TRUMAN J. SLUGHOUND, AS I LIVE BREATHE AND WHIZZ!"

Ant and Cleo turned to see Glenn Bob on his hands and knees, with his head down at floor level for no satisfactory reason. Glenn Bob was answered by a repulsive sucking sound from one of the airvents.

"HE DONE SLITHERED UP THEIR AIR CONDITIONING!" yelled Glenn Bob. "HE DONE FOUND YOU AGAIN!"

A dozen excited eyestalks pressed through the vent grille. Glenn Bob's caressing hand was covered in a thin coating of slime.

"Iffen these bars was plastic, Truman J. could bite through them quickeren stink", whispered Glenn Bob. "Mind, they ain't", he said. "They're steel. But iffen they was plastic - our Truman J. just loves a nice juicy piece of polypropylene."

"What, like that grille out there?" said Ant, pointing out through the cell door.

"Where?" Glenn Bob jumped up and bounced over to the window.

"That little one down by the desk in that corner. Same place as it is in this room. I suppose they made the bars out of steel in here because this is a prison cell. But I bet the air conditioning goes all the way from there to here."

Glenn Bob stared out through the glass, and began to smile. "Them bars is polypropylene all right. I'd know polypropylene anywhere."

"Great", said Cleo, eyeing the slithering horror through the vent grille distastefully. "Now all we have to do, as mentioned at length before, is get through a solid steel door."

13 - Air Conditioning Can Be Fun

"What are they d-doing out there?" chattered Cleo. The temperature was down again.

"N-not a lot", answered Ant. "They've finished the last of the wh-whisky. They're l-looking rather ill."

"Where's Comrade Furby?" said Cleo.

"On C-Captain Popov's d-desk console, j-just next to the d-door. The Captain d-doesn't seem to be h-here right now. P-probably interrogating s-someone else."

"Mr. T-Turpin, shouldn't wonder." Cleo shivered, not just from the cold.

"Th-that's f-fifteen t-times they've come into our c-cell now", said Ant. "C-Captain P-P-Popov's b-been talking to the F-Furby for hours at his d-desk."

"Th-then it's t-time", Cleo admitted, "to t-try out your moronic plan."

"H-how do I wake it up?"

"It won't h-hear you talking through the d-door. Bang the g-glass. It m-might h-hear that."

Outside the room, on Captain Popov's cluttered desk, the furby sat holding down a number of intelligence reports. In the dark and presumably quiet room outside, it appeared to have gone to sleep.

Carefully, experimentally, Ant raised a fist and rapped the glass lightly with his knuckles; nothing. Frustrated, he banged harder.

One of the Soviet guards turned over in his delirium, and mumbled. The furby's gigantic violet eyes flickered open. It stared into the dark through gorgeous eyelashes. Ant banged again.

Whether because of Ant's banging or because of the Russian soldiers' mumbling, the furby began to talk. What it was saying couldn't be heard, but all its plastic bits moved in just the way they should if the furby were talking audibly. Ant continued to bang. The furby continued to chatter to itself.

Cleo glared at Ant from her position curled up on the other side of the cell.

***

"We have carried out Yanalysis of syamples collyected at site of Croatoan atrocity", said Captain Popov. His eyes were bloodshot, and he was slouching in his chair. Ant suspected he had been helping his men to analyse samples of Croatoan moonshine.

Comrade Furby sat next to him on the metal desk. The furby was wearing a KGB officer's cap which was far too large for it. It was also wearing a KGB officer's jacket and epaulettes.

"Comrade Furby is wearing a Russian uniform", said Cleo.

"Yuniform is being myade spyecially for Comrade Fyurby by Lieutenant Christov, who is yexcellent syeamstress", said Captain Popov. "Sometimes, we are worrying about Lieutenant Christov", he added in a confiding whisper.

Cleo looked at the furby's shoulder flashes critically.

"Comrade Furby appears to outrank you", said Cleo.

Captain Popov smiled. He saluted the furby.

"Yis byest thying", he said. "A commanding officer who yissue no orders."

"Ah-may koh-koh", said the furby.

Captain Popov frowned. He levelled a finger at Ant and Cleo.

"Croatoan syamples yindicate", said the Captain, "yextraterrestrial DNA."

"You mean", said Cleo, "*alien* DNA?"

"Could be New Dixie DNA", said Ant. "New Dixie's got alien life by the pantload."

Captain Popov shook his head. "Yis not oryiginating in New Dyixieland, and yis not terryestrial either".

"You mean an *alien spaceship?*", said Glenn Bob, whose jaw had dropped.

"So?" Ant looked from Captain Popov to Glenn Bob. "What's so special about that? There are aliens on New Dixie. Truman J. Slughound is an ali-"

Cleo kicked Ant under the table. It hurt. A hideous slobbering sound came from the airvents. Glenn Bob stood up and sidled across the room, stopping to warm his hands on the ventilator grille, which was belching freezing cold air. Coincidentally, this stopped Captain Popov or the sentry from seeing the twenty-odd gastropod eyestalks poking curiously into the cell.

"Don't be stupid, Ant", said Cleo. "Everybody knows there's no intelligent alien life in space. Why, the Captain said so only yesterday."

"A few weeks ago", said Ant, "I knew there were no Americans on Alpha Centauri."

"Are no Yamericans on Alpha Centauri", said the Captain. "Alpha Centauri is star. Yis too hot for Yamericans." He looked at the Furby warily. "If yis true that syamples show yextraterrestrial origin, Croatoan is destroyed by Unknown Yalien Power. We have alryeady transmyitted myessage to Red Star Fleet indicating destruction of Croatoan by USZ. Is not true. I yapologize. When tyests on syamples are complyete, we transmyit warning to Fleet that Croatoan is destroyed by Yenemy Yaliens."

"Gosh", said Cleo. "Thank you for apologizing."

"Can we go now?" said Ant.

Captain Popov shook his head. "No. You have not told truth."

Ant blinked. Captain Popov was still there.

"But you just told us that Croatoan was destroyed by aliens", said Ant. Captain Popov, meanwhile, sat quiet on the other side of the table.

Ant and Cleo waited patiently. The Captain didn't move a muscle.

"Aha!" Cleo clicked her fingers. "I understand now. This is an example of communist doublethink. The Captain knows that Croatoan was destroyed by aliens, and will warn his own Fleet that this has happened, but it will advance the cause of Universal Communism if two enemy capitalist nations believe they've been attacked by each other. Therefore, the Captain would still like us, if I am not mistaken, to confess to the fact that the United States of the Zodiac attacked Croatoan. Am I right?"

The Captain's left eyebrow twitched a millimetre.

"Good. I am glad we understand each other", said Cleo, smiling sweetly. "Then, with the greatest respect, the Captain can walk north till his hat floats."

Captain Popov's face went red as the stars on his epaulettes with fury. He rose from the table and unsheathed his finger at Ant, Glenn Bob and Cleo.

"We know", said Cleo. "We will tell truth."

The Captain's face brightened suddenly. A half-smile formed itself on his features. "You will tell truth?" he said.

"No", said Cleo. "We will not tell truth."

The Captain grimaced. A clear sound of teeth grinding issued from him.

"Then you will starve", he said, rose from the desk, and left.

***

The cell was dark. Glenn Bob and Cleo shivered in one corner. Only Ant, rapping at the door's circular viewport, was not attempting to sleep - and only Ant, it seemed, was in any danger of drifting off.

Ant rapped on the glass with cold-whitened knuckles that the skin was fast vanishing from. It was dark in the Captain's office outside, but the window was covered with a thin rime of ice - ice on the wrong side of the glass. It was only possible to see whether anyone was awake beyond the glass if the ice melted, and in order to melt the ice, Ant had to press part of himself up against it and bore a hole with his body heat. With the heat in his face, he had made a hole small enough to see through, and could just make out the Captain's peak-capped head slumped in his chair, no doubt warm and cosy. The Captain appeared to be snoring, but Ant could take no chances. Each rap had to be tiny, measured, audible to nobody but the Furby. Whilst he rapped with the one hand, he breathed onto his other hand to warm it. He was rapidly losing the ability to feel his face -

And then both halves of the door hinged away and stowed themselves neatly into the walls.

Ant's success took him by surprise. The Captain grunted in his sleep as a small hurricane of hot air whooshed out of his office into the cell. Ant stood staring at the Captain for several seconds before turning and hissing *"Cleo! Glenn Bob!"*

"Gnufurm what is it now?"

"It worked...the cell door is now open."

Cleo jerked upright like a vampire rising from the dead. *"WHAT? Why didn't you TELL me -"*

"I am telling you, aren't I?"

"Magic! Now we can get out of here!"

Ant thought about this as he crossed the Captain's office as if walking a minefield. *"No we can't, Cleo."*

"What are you talking about? The bloody door is bloody open!"

Ant bent down to the ventilator grille. *"And where are we going to go after we get out of the door? This isn't some prison with walls and a world outside. This is a spaceship under thrust. If we get out of here they'll only search the ship from stem to stern, find us and drag us right back here again."* He tapped on the ventilator grille lightly. As he tapped, the Furby cooed back to him in Russian.

"Oh fine! Oh fantastic! We'll just not walk out of an open cell then, shall we?"

In the dark behind the grille, Ant's taps were answered by a hideous molluscoid gurgling. *"We don't just need a way to get out of the cell. We need a way to get into and out of it at any time we like, without being noticed."*

A forest of eyestalks grew out of the grille. Truman J. Slughound snuffled at the bars excitedly. *"Ah - good sluggie"*, said Ant. *"That's my fine sluggie there. Just you take a whiff of all that juicy polypropylene. I bet you'd love to get your choppers into that, wouldn't you?"*

Cleo stood in the doorway talking to Ant. *"Ant, what are you* doing *in there? We are supposed to be getting out of here, not feeding the local fauna - YIKE!"*

The two halves of the cell door had tried to snap back together smartly. Instead, they'd bounced back into the ceiling, and Ant looked up to see Glenn Bob stretched at full length in the doorway, staring at his hand as if he couldn't believe the door hadn't chopped it off at the wrist.

"Well, at least we know the safety circuits work" he whispered, to Cleo. *"Doors won't take your hand off there."*

The ventilator bars began to foam and steam as the sluggie tucked into them enthusiastically. Ant kept one eye on the Captain, who appeared to be having a bad dream in his sleep, which fortunately seemed to be keeping him from noticing the one that was happening right next to him in reality.

The Captain continued to snore.

"I don't think he'd wake up even if someone plugged him in the head with his own piece", whispered Glenn Bob, staring hungrily at the pistol in the Captain's belt.

"I am certain this is true", said Ant. *"But no-one is going to do such a thing. Are they."* He glared meaningfully at Glenn Bob.

Truman J. Slughound burped out a cloud of glacial acetic acid that took Ant's breath away. Ant wafted the cloud away from himself with his hand, then carefully lifted a handkerchief out of the Captain's top pocket, dabbed it with vodka from the open bottle on the table, put this over his nose and mouth and squeezed himself through the wrecked stumps of the bars into the ventilator.

"So I'll just stay in here like a lemon staring at an open door, shall I?" complained Cleo.

"No", came Ant's voice from out of the air conditioning. *"Actually, I need you to go out into the office and find me a screwdriver."*

Inside the ventilator, it was cold and dark. Small squares of light were visible along the walls. The nearest one, Ant reckoned, must be the steel-barred vent in the cell. Ant dragged himself towards it on knees and elbows. Just to add that final polish to things, inside of the duct was lavishly coated with Sluggie slime.

"And where", hissed Cleo irritably, *"am I going to find one of those?"*

"Look in the Captain's desk", whispered Ant. *"He's bound to have small sharp things for sticking into prisoners."*

Cleo tiptoed past Captain Popov, who was by now making gurgling noises that could have put Truman J. Slughound to shame, and pulled the desk drawer open with the care of a bomb disposal expert.

"Anything in there?" said Ant.

"Er - rocket pistol, snowstorm globe of the Kremlin, tube of something, 'мазь

Геморрой' *- probably toothpaste - spare pair of glasses - vodka - vodka - vodka -* " her hands clinked alarmingly as she searched the desk in the dark - *"aha! Soviet Army knife."* She raced very quietly into the cell and passed the knife through the grille. *"I don't know if it's got a screwdriver on it, mind."*

"Doesn't matter. I can use a knifeblade as a flat screwdriver if I have to." There was a sound of grunting and physical exertion that seemed to go on for some time.

Then, the ventilator grille popped clean out of the wall, tumbling toward the bare steel floor, and smacked solidly into the outstretched palm of Glenn Bob, who had somehow managed to dive back entirely silently across the whole length of the cell to field it, whilst still keeping one foot in the cell doorway. The cell doors attempted to shut round his shoe and bounced back up into the ceiling again.

Glenn Bob glared up at Cleo.

"Erm. Sorry", said Cleo, *"I really should have caught that myself, shouldn't I."*

"That's okay", whispered Glenn Bob. *"Girls kin't catch."*

"I'LL HAVE YOU KNOW THEY CAN - " started Cleo, but was interrupted by Ant.

"WHEN YOU TWO HAVE QUITE FINISHED, get back in the guardroom, shut the cell door, and come back through the ventilator into the cell. I want to make sure we can all fit down the ventilator."

"WHAT?" said Cleo.

"You heard me. Once we get back into the cell, we'll be able to move about inside the ship as we please through the ventilation system. Remember, we can't just get out of the cell and think we're free. This whole ship's one big prison as far as we're concerned."

"So how do we escape, then, if we can't leave the cell?" whispered Cleo contemptuously.

"We need to find two things", said Ant. *"First, we need to find a ship. You heard the Captain say this ship is a carrier. That must mean there are smaller ships on board it."*

"And the other thing?" said Cleo.

"We need to find Mr. Turpin", said Ant.

14 - Attack of the Pantbeast

The Captain looked from Ant to Cleo to Glenn Bob.

"You will explyain plyease", he said, "why you are covered in slime."

Glenn Bob turned to Cleo. Cleo turned to Ant.

"It's a rare medical condition", said Ant. "Native to New Dixie. It causes the body to secrete huge quantities of slime. It's called, er, Slime Disease."

"Did not hyave condyition when you fyirst cyame aboard", said the Captain suspiciously.

"We must have caught it in the swamps", said Ant. "Common in swamps, Slime Disease."

"Extremely common", said Cleo.

"Syimilar tryaces of slime have been found lyeading yinto one of our cyarrier's wheel wells", said Popov. "And several pairs of nylon pyants have vyanished from our starshyip laundry."

"Ah", said Ant. "That'll be a Linklater's Lesser Pant Eater, then."

"Pyant Yeater?" said Popov.

"A fearsome beast, native to the Slime Swamps of New Dixie", elaborated Ant. "Your men must have taken insufficient precautions, or it could never have come aboard. Normally it eats nylon, but it'll take polyester if it can get it. I advise all your men to go about unpanted until the beast is caught."

Cleo's face attempted to flicker into a smile, but she immediately froze it back into a poker-faced frown.

"How to cyatch byeast?" said Popov. He had taken out a notebook, and was writing it all down.

"Normally, they lair in lavatories and sewage systems", said Ant. "All the more easy to lie concealed in the inky depths of the S-bend, hoping to surface and rip the pants from the buttocks of an unsuspecting sitter."

"Yinky dyepths", said Captain Popov, scribbling. Cleo's face was going red, and she appeared to be attempting to chew her own lips.

"The best method of protection is to insist on natural fibre underpants only for your men. Wool-rich simply won't do", said Ant. "Linklater's Pant Eater can smell both fear and lycra. It's one hundred per cent cotton or nothing." Cleo's face had by now turned bright purple, and her cheeks were expanding like balloons about to pop.

The Captain finished scribbling, his tongue in the corner of his mouth. Then, he got up from the table, saluted, and scurried from the room. As he left, he turned and raised his finger to point menacingly at Ant.

"I will tell truth", said Ant obediently.

"Good", said Captain Popov, and left.

"Правда!", said the sentry sternly, and closed the door.

Cleo exploded, collapsing onto the floor in hysterics before the chair had even had time to vanish into the floor.

"What?" said Glenn Bob. "That Linklater's Pant Eater stuff, was that not entirely true there?"

***

It was pitch dark inside the steel duct, and slimy. Truman J. Slughound, who had made the duct slimy, was also interesting himself in the plastic soles of Ant's trainers.

What can you see? said Cleo from behind him. Ant felt himself wishing it had been Cleo, not Glenn Bob, who had stayed behind in the cell. *It's not another store cupboard, is it?*

Through the grille, Ant could vaguely make out a dimly lit, cavernous chamber that was definitely not a store cupboard. Arranged along a steel deck that stretched and stretched and stretched into the distance, he could see huge, sleek saucer shapes - not the dumpy, big-bellied space runabout Mr. Turpin had abducted them from Earth in, but razor-edged, shark-finned things that seemed to be travelling at warp speed even when they were standing still.

Of course, Ant reminded himself, the entire vessel was already travelling at warp speed, so the ships on the other side of the grille *were* actually moving, even if Ant was moving at the same speed as they were.

"What have you found?" said Cleo, attempting to squirm past Truman J. Slughound - an unwise move, as the fur fringe on her anorak hood could be made of nothing other than nylon.

"Fighters", said Ant. "We've found a fighter hangar."

Cleo inched up to the grille and squinted through it.

"Pah!" she said. "Those are no good. They don't have enough seats for us all. Where's Mr. Turpin going to sit?"

"There are two seats on those ones. Pilot and navigator, probably. That one's got its canopy back, look. And two of us could probably fit into one of those seats. They're made for big fat full-grown Communists -"

"If you think I'm sitting on your lap all the way to Earth you've got another think coming, buster. And what about Glenn Bob?"

Ant couldn't think of an answer. Glenn Bob had been prepared to stay in the cell indefinitely to keep Mr. Turpin alive. It didn't seem right to abandon him.

"What about that one?" he said, pointing across the hangar.

"That's the same model as all the others."

"No it isn't. Look at the canopy. There's an extra seat. It's probably a training model, with another cockpit for the instructor."

"If you say so."

"It might not have any weapons on board, mind."

"I want to get away from these people, Ant, not shoot them."

"All right then. We're agreed. All we have to do now is find Mr. Turpin."

***

Mr. Turpin's cell was similar to their own. He was lying in a corner with his face to the wall. He had curled into a ball, hugging his hands under his armpits with his legs folded up beneath him. The air in the room made Ant's breath steam as he looked through the grille.

"Can you see him?" said Cleo. "Is he alive?"

"I think so", said Ant. "The ice on the cell floor's melted around him." He pulled his head back from the ventilator. "Ough! Ny tongue froze to ge ngetal!"

"What's he doing right now?" said Cleo.

"Shivering", said Ant.

"Useless nincompoop", said Cleo. "Why doesn't he just tell them what they want?"

"What, so they can shoot him once they don't need him any more?" said Ant.

"They wouldn't shoot him", said Cleo, in a voice that sounded less sure than she intended. "I mean, he must know lots about enemy military spaceships and stuff. They'd be sure to keep him alive."

"So he can get his comrades killed", said Ant.

"Given a choice between getting my comrades killed and getting killed myself, I'll get my comrades killed every time", said Cleo.

"I'll bear that in mind", said Ant.

Suddenly, the grille flicked open in front of Ant with a deafening roar, making him completely visible to anyone in the cell. Ant panicked. Yelping, he sprang further back into the ventilator, colliding with Cleo. The air in the vent was also, suddenly, searingly hot.

"I CAN'T BREATHE", screamed Cleo. "I CAN'T BREATHE I CAN'T BREATHE I CAN'T BREATHE", she added.

"IF YOU CAN YELL, YOU CAN BREATHE", yelled Ant. "BACK UP SLOWLY AND LET'S GET OUT OF HERE."

***

They dropped out of the ventilator back into blissful freezing cold. Glenn Bob was shivering bitterly, but despite this, had the vent cover back on its screws in the wall almost before Ant and Cleo's feet had hit the ground.

"Why'd you think they're turning the heat up in Mr. Turpin's cell?" said Cleo.

"It was colder in that cell than they ever made it in here", said Ant. "Well below freezing. He couldn't stand that for long without it killing him. They're freezing and frying him every hour or so, I shouldn't wonder, to try and break him."

"He deserves it", said Cleo, "the filthy kidnapper."

"PSSSST!" said Glenn Bob. "PSSSST, there!" Ant and Cleo looked in the direction Glenn Bob was frantically jerking his head. The ice rime on the outside of the cell door had been wiped away, and the sentry's face was beaming in. He waved cheerily. Ant and Cleo put on gigantic plastic smiles and waved back.

The sentry opened the door. Captain Popov entered with great ceremony, stamping his feet against the cold. The sentry blew on his hands to warm them as he moved to stand guard by the table which was rising from the floor.

Ant and Cleo grinned enormous guilty mouths full of teeth at Captain Popov. Ant's heart was drumming thrash metal in his chest.

Captain Popov sat down. But he looked up suspiciously at Ant and Cleo, who were sitting bolt upright at the table, then peered round them at Glenn Bob, who was still shivering uncontrollably.

"You do not feel cold?" he said to Ant and Cleo.

"Oh no", said Ant, and added confidingly: "We're British, you see."

Glenn Bob glared at Ant, and sneezed violently.

***

The ventilator grille dropped out of the wall, but did not hit the ground; two sets of shoelaces wrapped around it had stopped it falling far.

The cell was like a sauna. Ant writhed carefully through the ventilator to prevent any exposed flesh touching bare metal. The cell door was misted with condensation on the inside, which was good. Any guard wanting to take a look inside would have to physically open the door.

Mr. Turpin was huddled in the same position Ant had last seen him in, facing the wall, not moving. Ant had no idea whether he was even breathing.

"*Psssst!*" whispered Ant. "*Mr. Turpin!*" Then, remembering that the cell was soundproofed, he walked over to the prisoner and yelled "COOOEEEE! MR. TURPIN!"

He shook the man by the shoulder. Mr. Turpin did not reply. Ant shook him again.

"Now, look here, sleeping beauty", said Ant, growing more than a little annoyed, "we've come a long way to get you out of here. Over twenty yards, in fact. The least you could do is -"

Mr. Turpin's head turned round to stare in Ant's direction. His eyes boggled moronically. Blood and drool trailed out of one corner of his mouth. The shape of his face could only be made out dimly past the mass of bruises that covered it. Blood, Ant noticed, was also puddled around his fingertips on the floor.

"Oh dear", said Ant.

"*What's the matter?*" hissed Cleo from the airvent.

"There's no need to whisper", said Ant. "The cell's soundproof. I don't think Mr. Turpin can walk."

"The USELESS IDIOT! We should leave him here to FRY! And freeze, of course."

"And who's going to fly our saucer out of here then?"

"Glenn Bob can fly a saucer", said Cleo.

"I can too", agreed Glenn Bob.

"Glenn Bob was also able to find us a working radio transmitter and get us across country to Roanoke. Do you see a pattern developing here?"

Glenn Bob said nothing, but sat back hard against the walls of the ventilator, making the metal clang.

"Now he's sulking", said Ant.

"Well, as long as you aren't sulking too, you can help me shift him out of here into the ventilator. Whether it's him or Glenn Bob who flies the ship, if this man stays here he's going to die."

"Oh, all right then." Cleo unfolded herself from the airvent, took hold of Mr. Turpin's legs and made as if to drag him across the floor with effortless ease. This approach did not work. "Ungkk. He's too heavy, Ant."

Ant looked up into the ventilator. "Glenn Bob", he said, "we need your help."

Glenn Bob frowned, then nodded.

"He'll die iffen he stays here, I reckon", he said, spat on his hands, and jumped down into the cell.

Even with the three of them working together, it was a struggle to fit Mr. Turpin into the duct. His shoulders only just squeezed through the narrow opening. Also, he didn't appear to have worked out what was happening to him, and fought back weakly, so that Ant was forced to pinch his fingertips hard until he squealed and stopped.

"That seemed to shut him up", said Cleo. "What did you do?"

"Erm", said Ant. "I'm not entirely sure he still has fingernails on two of his hands. I reckoned the wounds might still be sensitive."

Cleo went pale and put her hand over her mouth.

"Not in here, please", said Ant.

Mr. Turpin was, however, eventually stuffed into the vent, where he moaned and dribbled while Ant and Glenn Bob pushed him up the tube from behind and Cleo pulled him by the shoulders from the front. Luckily, the walls of the vent had been well lubricated by Truman J. Slughound, who raced ahead of them all at a snail's pace. Unfortunately, this also meant that it was difficult to get a firm footing to push and pull against.

"GRAAAAH!" grunted Cleo. "You are the most GOOD FOR NOTHING man I have ever had to pull up an air conditioning unit - NNK - can't you even help a *little*?"

"*BE QUIET, Cleo*", hissed Ant. "*You're making more noise than he is.*"

Thankfully, Mr. Turpin was making considerably less noise by the time he had been pushed halfway across the ship on his way to the fighter hangar. In fact, Ant was not entirely sure he wasn't *enjoying* being pushed.

"*Shouldn't we have made cardboard models of ourselves and left them in the cell or something*?" said Cleo.

"*Somehow I don't think even Captain Popov would have been fooled*", said Ant. "*We've just got to get to the hangar before someone opens either our cell or Mr. Turpin's.*"

"*And get this bag of bones to snap out of it enough to fly a ship out of here for us*", reminded Cleo.

"*Maybe Glenn Bob can fly us the first light year or so*", said Ant airily. "*Try and slap some sense into Turpin in the meantime.*"

There was a sound of enthusiastic slapping from further up the duct.

"*WITHOUT ACTUALLY KILLING HIM*", clarified Ant.

After a few more minutes' shoving, Mr. Turpin had arrived at the grille in the wall of the hangar. Having pushed him further on into the vent, Glenn Bob and Ant peered through the ventilator into the darkened chamber.

"*Result*", breathed Ant. "*No lights on, nobody at home. D'you think you can fly one of those things?*"

Glenn Bob looked at the enormous, razor-edged war saucers with trepidation. "*Don't know rightly. I can try sure enough.*"

This was good enough for Ant, who ushered Truman J. Slughound up to the bars. "*There's a good sluggie. Look at all that yummy polypropylene.* Doesn't *that look good.*"

Turning crimson and purple with pleasure, the sluggie set to devouring the bars. Before long, the ventilator grille was a mass of twisted stumps.

"*GOOD sluggie there*", beamed Glenn Bob in encouragement. "*That's a good polymerivore there, boy.*"

Truman J. Slughound burped out an asphyxiating cloud of glacial acetic acid and rubbed himself affectionately across Glenn Bob's face.

Mr. Turpin protested feebly as he was dragged out of the ventilator across the bubbling remnants of the bars. He seemed to be trying to help Ant and Glenn Bob walk him across the hangar towards the line of fighters, but appeared to have no strength in his legs.

"*Which one?*" whispered Cleo as they scurried under the gigantic, menacing craft. "*They all look the same.*"

"*That one*", said Ant, pointing.

"*How do we get into it?*"

The saucer was very big, very solid, and was made of a great deal of steel.

"*Erm*", said Ant.

Having found a ladder that led through the blade-thin wing of the saucer onto its back, Glenn Bob climbed up it.

"*Oh, for goodness' sake*", said Cleo. "*Just smash the window and undo the door from the inside.*"

Up above, Ant's head, Glenn Bob began fiddling with the canopy glass.

"*If all goes well*", spat Ant, "*this ship will be in a perfect vacuum in five minutes' time. How clever will smashing the glass have been then, Einstein?*"

"*It's open*", said Glenn Bob.

"*What?*" said Ant and Cleo together.

"*Wasn't locked*", said Glenn Bob. "*Didn't* got *no lock, I think.*"

"*NO LOCK?*" Ant was climbing up behind Glenn Bob, goggling at him as he climbed into the open cockpit.

"*This here is a military aircraft*", said Glenn Bob, "*in a military hangar. Who's going to steal it?*"

"*What, apart from us, you mean?*" said Cleo cuttingly.

Ant shrugged. "*I suppose this* is *deep space*", he said, "*not Toxteth.*" He jumped down the ladder and began to heave Mr. Turpin towards it. "*Come and give us a hand here.*"

Mr. Turpin was extremely heavy, and Glenn Bob and Cleo both had to help lift him up the ladder. Eventually he was dumped unceremoniously over the lip of the cockpit into a rather uncomfortable-looking pilot's seat, where he stared bemused at the instruments, moving his hands over them like a child just set down in a new nursery. Ant, meanwhile, made sure Mr. Turpin's arms and legs were all inside the cockpit and tried to buckle him in to the seat.

"*This is* my *seat*", said Cleo, settling grandly into the navigator's seat behind Mr. Turpin.

"*Hey*", complained Glenn Bob from the rear cockpit. "*This console's all in Commie.*"

Mr. Turpin, meanwhile, was fingering the banks of dials and switches like a pyromaniac in a fireworks factory. A dim light of understanding seemed to be dawning in his eyes. Ant slapped his hands away from the controls irritably, and clambered round the vessel to the navigator's seat.

"*Ohhhh no*", said Cleo. "*You're not sitting in HERE, buster.*"

"*Suit yourself*", said Ant. "*I'll sit with Glenn Bob.*"

"*Huh?*" said Glenn Bob.

"*Of course*", said Ant, "*that means* you'll *be sitting with Truman J. Slughound.*" On cue, a battery of eyestalks slithered over the edge of Cleo's cockpit. Cleo recoiled in horror.

"Ugh! Ugh! Get away from me, you minging mollusc!"

"Still want to sit in there on your own?" said Ant sweetly.

"Okay! Okay! But I sit on you, not the other way round. You weigh a ton."

Ant clambered back to the navigator's seat. Truman J. Slughound, rebuffed, glided across the saucer and poured himself into Glenn Bob's seat.

"Good sluggie! That's my fine slughound, there!"

The canopy began closing over Ant and Cleo's heads.

"I think I found the canopy button, y'all", commented Glenn Bob's voice from speakers in the console. *"Now I'm looking for the main reaction drive. That'll send us to point one of lightspeed in a bag of jiffies."*

"Shouldn't we be outside *the carrier",* said Ant, *"before we turn on the main drive?"*

There was a pause. Glenn Bob's voice came back from the console.

"Ahhm, you may have yourself a point there."

"Then where", said Cleo, looking round the hangar, *"is the exit?"*

"Can't see no door anywhere in these four walls", said the console dispiritedly, and then suddenly added: *"Ah."*

"Clarify 'Ah'", said Ant.

"Look up."

Ant looked up. Casting an immense shadow over the fighter saucers parked in the hangar was a colossal mountain of machinery. Resting on a mass of pipes, cables and pillars, it was the source of a gigantic pipe that led away from it in a straight line right through the hangar wall, and in one side of it, Ant could make out an enormous door with giant red letters picked out on its surface spelling Запустить Пушка.

"What does 'Запустить Пушка ' mean?" said Cleo into the console.

"I'll take a guess at 'Launch Gun', the console replied.

"Launch *Gun",* said Cleo, in a voice that sounded not entirely happy with this.

"Sure", said Glenn Bob. *"These here big military carriers launch their fighter complement into space out of big steam cannon. The biggest ones can fire a wing of fighters a minute. It is perfectly safe and normal",* he added reassuringly. Cleo's face did not look reassured.

"That's the door?" said Ant.

"It's a door", said Glenn Bob's voice.

"How do we get up there?"

"No idea", said the console. *"Maybe iffen I just fly straight at it, it'll just open straight on up - GIT DOWN LOWEREN A SLUGGIE'S BELLY!"*

Glenn Bob's head disappeared into his cockpit canopy. Ant and Cleo tried vainly to squirm further down into their own seat, fighting each other for space. Cleo elbowed Ant in the ribs. Ant pulled Cleo's hair extensions. But then they both froze in mid-elbow and mid-pull.

The personnel door to the hangar was trembling open, screeching like a scalded cat sliding down a blackboard. Evidently the doors in the hangar area were not as well oiled as the doors to the KGB cells.

Light flooded into the hangar. Gigantic arc lights blazed into life up above them. Through the corner of his eye, Ant saw the silhouette of a sentry saluting a squad of Russian officers walking into the chamber. The officers were being led by a red-faced man with a moustache like the tusks of a white walrus, who was gesticulating excitedly at the fighters, making zooming gestures with the palms of his hands. Ant guessed that this must be the officer in charge of the fighter squadron, showing off his toys to his commanding officers. The commanding officers, old men to a man, strode about stiffly, nodding as if they understood every word of what was being said to them. The fighter commander was walking closer along the line of saucers, pointing out the differences between each, getting perilously close to the machine in which Ant, Cleo, Glenn Bob, Mr. Turpin, and J. Truman Slughound were hiding. *If they even* glance *at this machine,* thought Ant, *or look at the ventilator missing from the wall....*

Meanwhile, at the other end of the hangar, the sentry on duty at the door paced round in bored circles, his rocket rifle on his shoulder. Ant realised with a sinking heart that this was the same sentry who had stood guard outside their cell.

Then, at one point, the sentry turned his head as he paced, and looked Ant straight in the eye, and - Ant was not even sure it had actually happened - winked. Then he got back to his pacing.

The officers turned round and headed back towards the door, not before one of the more senile-looking ones had smiled and waved at Mr. Turpin, who was grinning and dribbling at them from his own cockpit. The other officers, luckily, seemed not to have seen Mr. Turpin. They walked out of the hangar, and the sentry saluted and closed the door behind them.

Then, he relaxed, stood at ease, and turned to look directly at the training fighter once again.

"*He knows we're here*", whispered Cleo.

Ant made a decision, and felt round the base of the cockpit canopy until he found what he thought was the release mechanism. He pressed it, and the canopy glass hissed open and rose up. Ant clambered across the back of the saucer and down the ladder leading through it to the hangar floor. He walked up to the sentry, stood to attention, and saluted.

The sentry made a big show of standing to attention and saluting back. "Доброе Утро, Товарищ ", he said.

"You're letting us go", said Ant.

"We are not all KGB", said the sentry. "My brother, he is in *gulag* because of KGB."

"What's a gulag?" said Ant, who was horribly sure it was a sort of meat stew.

The soldier laughed. "Gulag is byeautiful communist hyoliday cyamp", he said. He looked across the hangar at a CCTV camera mounted on a beam, and waved at it happily.

"Won't waving at that camera get you into terrible trouble?" said Ant, looking at the camera in alarm. The soldier shook his head. "Cyameras do not work. Spyare parts are not arryiving from fyactory." He raised a finger to Ant, as if to say, *wyait a myinute*, and walked across the hangar to a kit bag stuck to the floor with velcro. He lifted something out of the bag and handed it to Ant. It was Comrade Furby.

"You were going to yescape without yimportant myember of your tyeam, yes?" he said, beaming.

"You knew we were going to escape", said Ant, flabbergasted.

The soldier nodded and smiled guiltily. "But yis no ryeason to tyell our Cyaptain Popov, yes?" He set the Furby down on the deck and saluted it smartly. Ant, grinning, gathered it up.

"I adjyourn this myeeting of the Byanana Splyits Clyub", said the sentry. "Don't you all be cyoming back now."

"We would love not to come back", said Ant, "but we can't figure out how to fly out of the airlock." He pointed up at the massive bulk of the fighter launcher.

"Is all syet up for lyaunch", said the sentry. "You dryive fyighter skyids into cyatapult slyed." He pointed across the room at a low platform which looked like a pallet truck mounted on a rail. "Then wheels yinterlock, cyatapult mechanyism loads fyighter into take-off bay, and Поехали!" The soldier banged his palm with his fist. "Is ten gee, very fast."

"Thank you", said Ant. He saluted again. "'Size of an Elephant'", he said.

The trooper saluted back. "'Size of an Yelephant'", he repeated.

Ant walked back across the hangar to the saucer, and climbed back into the cockpit. "We have to fly the skids of the fighter into that thing on the floor", he explained. Glenn Bob shrugged, activated whatever control closed Ant and Cleo's canopy, and saluted the sentry politely. Then, he confidently selected something to turn on the engines. The ship shuddered violently and began to vibrate hard enough to jar Ant's eyeballs.

"D'you think that's the Main Drive?" said Cleo.

"I think it might be Boil Wash", said Ant.

"*Think I got the impeller rolling on neutral there*", said Glenn Bob from the console, and there was a loud CLUNK of levers being thrown. The ship growled like a bull with a cowboy it didn't like sitting on its back, and began shuddering so hard Ant could not see the Russian characters on the console, much less understand them.

"And that'll be Rinse and Spin", said Ant.

"*Whoopsidaisy there*", said Glenn Bob. The thrumming stopped, and was replaced by a gentler roar. Ant realised suddenly that the hangar walls were moving down around them, and the ceiling was coming closer.

"Well done, that man", said Ant.

"*Okeydokey*", came Glenn Bob's voice. "*Now to nose her forward and down a smidgeon into that launching jig.*" The ship began to rise higher and move backward. "*Dangblasted Commie controls*", complained Glenn Bob, "*Let's try us that manoeuvre in the diametric opposite direction.*"

The ship stopped in mid-air and began slowly to move down and forwards. Ant heard one of the light fittings in the ceiling explode as the ship's fins touched it. The floor came up, glacially slowly. The fighter's landing skid nosed about on the floor for the launching sled while Glenn Bob pseudo-blasphemed again and again at his controls.

Then the skid connected. The whole saucer slammed down suddenly on the deck with a CLANG that shook Ant's teeth like tuning forks. Then the ship lifted, as if on a giant escalator, and began to move across the hangar toward the sliding door in the side of the Launch Gun, which started to creak ponderously open.

"That airlock chamber's tiny", commented Cleo.

"*Tiny like a case round a bullet*", said Glenn Bob. "*Hold on to your hair there.*"

Ant turned round again to wave at the sentry, and caught a glimpse of the personnel door to the hangar closing, just as the Launch Gun door closed over the hangar and locked so tightly shut that Ant could hear the air squeal out of the join.

"*Mooooo*", said Mr. Turpin's voice happily through the intercom.

And then, Ant saw only bright white light, and heard only Glenn Bob's voice yelling "*YEEEEEEEEEHA!*" before the universe went out.

When he woke up, he was in space.

15 - Man Can't Live At This Speed

An alarm was sounding. Voices were yelling at Ant through the intercom in Russian. Star trails were spinning round him. He was suffocating in a tiny space because of someone who was sitting on his chest, stopping him from freeing himself by pushing open the glass above his hands. Somewhere around the edges of the glass, he knew, was a catch which would open it and let him out. He searched for it frantically with his fingers.

"ANT! ANT! STOP TRYING TO PUSH THE CANOPY OPEN! THIS IS CLEO!"

He realised suddenly why there were stars spinning round him. Cleo's breath was hot on his face.

"GLENN BOB!" he yelled. "STOP THE SHIP SPINNING! TURN ON THE MAIN DRIVE! GET US OUT OF HERE!"

"*I'M TRYING!*" came a deafening shout from the intercom. Turning his head with difficulty, Ant could see a crowd of eyestalks perched on Glenn Bob's head as he searched frantically through the banks of dials and switches in the instructor's cockpit.

"Oh dear", said Ant. "It's all going Horribly Wrong."

"*GOT IT*", yelled Glenn Bob unnecessarily. The ship seemed to straighten, and the stars to stand still. Cleo was no longer pressed against Ant's chest like a sack of potatoes. The fighter was drifting in mid-space.

Before Ant had actually been in space, he had somehow expected it to look like a starry night on Earth. When Mr. Turpin's ship had taken off, however, there had been no stars, just a glaring sun blotting out all other light. But here, there were bright glowing clouds of gas and dust laid across the universe like lengths of velvet. Ant, who had never properly seen the Milky Way, had been eagerly awaiting his first view of it from space - but here, there seemed to be no Milky Way either. Instead, the whole of space here seemed to be one big Milky Way, surrounding him with huge, painfully bright stars and lumps of tumbling iron that he thought might be asteroids, but some of which glowed as if they'd just been torn off a volcano.

"We're back in hyperspace", said Ant. "Oh no. We must have left the carrier while it was still in hyperspace."

"*Looks like hyperspace all right*", said Glenn Bob. "*This universe is real small and hot, and expanding fast.*"

"Is hyperspace smaller than our universe?" said Ant.

"*Certainly is. Otherwise, there'd be no point in going through it, would there? We zip through hyperspace to save us all that trouble of flying from here to Alpha Centauri there. Hyperspace is like a ping pong ball in the middle of a baseball, the baseball being our universe. We can go round the baseball to get from point A to point B, or we can burrow down to the ping pong ball and make the journey shorter. That's your simple four dimensional geometry.*"

"Oh", said Ant. "So smaller universes expand faster, do they?"

"*Yup. Our own universe was real small just after the Big Bang when God did all of his Creation. It's just got bigger since then.*"

"Glenn Bob", said Cleo, as if she had thought of something extremely unpleasant, "does this ship have a faster-than-light drive?"

Ant could see Glenn Bob looking round the cockpit. "*Don't look like it*", he concluded. "*Most fighters are too small to have hyperdrives.*"

"So we're stuck here", said Cleo. "We can't leave hyperspace. We are stranded here forever."

Almost on cue, two identical Russian military saucers dropped out of nowhere to flank their own fighter. The Russian voices became louder and more insistent in the console. A lump of cratered rock the size and shape of the Isle of Wight tumbled past overhead.

Then the console changed both voice and language and said: "*THIS IS CYAPTAIN GREGOR GREGOROVICH POPOV OF THE SOVIET ASSYAULT CYARRIER* ALEXEI STAKHANOV. *YOU WILL CYEASE YOUR*

YINTERSTELLAR PYIRACY AND RETURN BYEAUTIFUL SOVIET SPYACE FYIGHTER TO DOCK OR WE WYILL BE FORCED TO RYESORT TO TYOTAL YANNIHILATION OF YOURSYELVES OVER."

The two saucers flanking them were keeping pace with effortless ease.

"CAN'T WE OUTRUN THEM?" yelled Ant desperately into the console microphone.

"*Uh, that's a negatory*", came the reply. *"Them guys looks like they know a deal more about piloting these here machines than yours truly."*

"Such as knowing how to turn the main drive on?" said Ant sarcastically.

"*You could say that*", said the console forlornly. Then, it added, in Captain Popov's voice, "*YIS NO YESCAPE. YOU WILL SUBMYIT TO ADDYITION OF TOW CLYAMP PLYEASE."*

A long metal cable had snaked out of one of the flanking fighters, and was motoring slowly towards them, apparently under its own power. The tip of it was venting a blue flame like a rocket motor.

"Yis no Yescape", parroted Cleo hopelessly.

Ant's attention, however, was elsewhere. Rather than staring at the tow cable as it jetted closer, his eyes were fixed on Mr. Turpin.

Mr. Turpin, in the pilot's cockpit in front of Ant, was still examining the flight console in front of him, and Ant doubted he'd taken his eyes off it since he was first dumped into the pilot's seat. He'd stopped running his hands over the controls like a child in a new nursery, and was now sitting studying them carefully, as if imagining which did what.

"Look at him, doing nothing", said Cleo contemptuously.

Then, rapidly and without a single pause for thought, Mr. Turpin reached up above him and flicked several switches to the 'ON' position. Immediately, banks of lights that had been lit up in scarlet on the pilot's console streamed into green. Mr. Turpin reached forward, turned a second switch, and ignored the three-dimensional display that bounced into the glass screen in front of him, because by then he was busy flicking other switches, making the navigator's console in front of Ant and Cleo light up as bright a dense thicket of Christmas trees. In the three-dimensional display, a big green dot that Ant assumed was their own fighter was surrounded by one big green dot and two small ones, which Ant assumed were the Russian carrier and the two other fighters.

Then Mr. Turpin took hold of the joystick.

The universe turned inside out and upside down. Ant felt Cleo attempting to crush the life out of first one side of his chest, then the other. Stars that had stayed put a moment ago now moved so fast they became long and thin like string. An asteroid big as Bedfordshire whirled past Ant's ear so close, he could see craters inside its craters. In the console, a Russian voice was yelling, and there were red letters flashing on the display saying Враждебная Ракета! Then Mr. Turpin's hand moved again, and Ant was treated to an extra special close-up view of the universe as his face was jammed hard against the canopy glass. Star trails seared past his face. A bright white line slashed the dark like a lightsabre, and Ant knew it was the trail of an incoming missile. Then the cockpit turned upside down - or right side up, there was no up or down in space - and Ant was looking up straight into the eyes of a clearly terrified Russian fighter saucer pilot. The other ship was right above them, flying the wrong way up. The Russian pilot jinked desperately on his joystick left and right, but Mr. Turpin matched him jink for jink. The two men's eyes stayed locked. The Russian stared into Mr. Turpin's eyes, almost as if pleading. Then he began yelling into a microphone clipped to his flight helmet, and Ant saw a red dot blinking in the three-dimensional display inside his cockpit.

Then Mr. Turpin pulled hard on the stick and pirouetted away from the other ship, and Ant just had time to see the Russian's face fill with relief as he punched down hard on something in his cockpit and the entire front of his fighter blew away into space, carrying him away from his vessel just as *something* bright white and fiery tore into it from underneath and the saucer exploded into a galaxy of tiny fragments.

"*Clever*", breathed Glenn Bob. "*Real clever. He done hid his ship beneath the Russkie's, and the missile the other Commie fired homed in on his comrade."*

"Clever?" said Cleo. "He just nearly *killed* someone."

"*That someone was fixing to kill him*", reminded Glenn Bob. "*And us. And Turpin done rolled us out of the way to let him get to his eject in time.*"

Then the ship was moving again, and Ant and Cleo were crushing the life out of each other. The saucer raced through a sliver of light between two rolling boulders the size of Snowdonia.

Ant peered past Mr. Turpin at a blue glowing dot in the 3-D display on the pilot's panel. "He's still behind us", he said.

The stars turned like a glowing whirlpool as the ship veered and spun to escape invisible attacks from behind. Although the attacks were invisible, they were very real, as Ant could see when their ship scooted across the front of a planetoid which lit up in a line of sparkling flashes as they passed.

"What's the other ship trying to do to us, Glenn Bob?" said Ant.

"*Shoot little bitty slivers of ferrous metal up our butts*", said Glenn Bob informatively. "*They zip along right fast, about point zero one of lightspeed.*"

"Not lasers, then", said Ant.

"*What's a laser?*" said Glenn Bob.

"Nothing", said Ant. "That's a relief", he said to Cleo. "No lasers."

"Ant, those little bitty slivers of metal look like they made a hole the size of Godzilla's bum in that asteroid."

"Oh."

The ship raced under another asteroid, did a back flip over it that Ant was sure had left his eyeballs plastered to the canopy, and raced back in the opposite direction. Looking back, Ant saw a fizzing green star that had to be the pursuing fighter rounding the planetoid on a course that implied the enemy pilot had temporarily lost track of their ship. Then another tumbling hulk of space pumice blocked off the line of sight between them and the enemy fighter, and Ant was sure that this was no coincidence. Their ship was slowing, racing towards a third asteroid, which glowed in two colours as it tumbled toward them in the dark. One side of the rock fragment was reflecting the bright white light from the nearest star, almost as colourless as moonlight. But the dark half of the asteroid also glowed, with a dimmer, greenish-purple light that didn't look entirely healthy. It was here that their saucer murmured and burbled to a halt, with a squillion tons of emerald and violet turning slowly above their heads.

"Why does it glow?" said Cleo.

"*Natural fluorescence*", said Glenn Bob. "*Real clever. This asteroid's made of some sort of stuff that's luminous, maybe even radioactive. It'll hide our exhaust from that other fighter's sensors.*"

Mr. Turpin was looking up at the giant grinding mass of interstellar granite rotating above their heads. Occasionally, he would make an adjustment to the ship's controls without looking down, like a footballer trying to keep a billion-tonne ball in the air above him. Whenever he touched the controls the ship would drift forwards, backwards or sideways slightly with a whoosh of jets.

"*He's keeping the planetoid between us and that other fighter*", said Glenn Bob.

Russian voices began crackling out of the console once again. To begin with, the voices were quite loud, and then they began to fade, until eventually they could hardly be heard at all. When they had died away almost to nothing, Mr. Turpin sat back in his seat with one hand on the dog tag round his neck, raised the dog tag to his teeth, and bit down on it hard so that it snapped in half. In the gloom of the pilot's cockpit, a tiny red light could be seen winking inside the broken metal. Mr. Turpin settled back in his seat with a beatific smile, and went to sleep.

"I think", breathed Ant, "that we have just found out what Mr. Turpin is good at."

"Oh, yes, he's brilliant", said Cleo. "We die when the air supply runs out."

"No we don't", said Ant. "Don't you see? It's a, its a homing signal. He had a homing beacon hidden in his dog tag. It's probably sending out a signal to a USZ ship right now."

"Sorry to fart in your airlock", said Glenn Bob, *"but that ain't possible. We're in hyperspace. Ships in normal space can't pick up radio signals out of hyperspace."*

"So why did he even bother to activate the signal?" said Ant.

"Probly thinks he's still back in realspace. He's delirious."

"So we're going to die anyway. After all this."

"Sure does look that way."

"What are the symptoms of oxygen starvation?" said Cleo.

"Uh, shortness of breath", panted Glenn Bob. *"And listlessness",* he added, yawning.

"Couldn't we rig up some sort of enormous greenhouse to recycle our breath into oxygen?" said Cleo. "Plants breathe in carbon dioxide and breathe out oxygen, you know."

"You got yourself a seed nursery in your pants pocket there, do you?" said Glenn Bob.

"There's no need to be offensive", sighed Cleo.

Ant, meanwhile, was still staring over Mr. Turpin's shoulder. "Glenn Bob - what does it mean when something blinks red on the pilot's 3-D display, do you think?"

Glenn Bob thought for a moment. *"Means an enemy ship within target range, I shouldn't wonder",* he yawned.

"But the Russian ships that fired on us were green on the display."

"That's cause we was Russian, and they was Russian too. Ant, iffen you don't mind me saying, on occasion, you is a low watt bulb."

"So...if there *was* a red light on the display, that would mean a *non*-Russian ship, very close by", said Ant.

Glenn Bob thought again. He heaved out an enormous sigh. *"Guess so...d'you got such a light?"*

Cleo pushed Ant aside and gawped into the pilot's cockpit. "Yes! Yes! Yes, we do! I mean, we have! There's a ship coming to fetch us! Oh, happy day, callooh, callay, we're *saved*!"

"All we know bout that vessel", cautioned Glenn Bob, *"is that it ain't Russian."*

"That's good enough for me!" yelled Cleo. "Woohoo! Woohoo! Yahoo!" she added.

"Going 'woohoo woohoo yahoo' wastes oxygen", said Glenn Bob.

Through the canopy glass, meanwhile, Ant could see one more star than he'd been able to before - and that star was growing larger.

The radio squawked into life. *"Attention Soviet Mikoyan-Korolev. This is the United States of the Zodiac cruiser* Jervis Bay. *Do you require assistance, over?"*

"English", said Ant in disbelief.

"All the U.S. Zee speak English", said Glenn Bob breathily.

"No", said Ant. "He *is* English. Just like us and Mr. Turpin."

The star had by now grown large enough to be, visibly, a saucer under power. It was not a red-star-spangled monster like the Russian carrier, but was far smaller, not much larger than the U.S. Corvette *Virginia*. There were, though, as it came closer, a few stars on its hull - old ones that someone had tried to paint out and failed. An attempt had also been made to paint out the 'A' of 'USA' on its hull and replace it with a 'Z'.

Glenn Bob scoffed. *"Why, that ain't but one of our old* Revere *class light cruisers with a different paintjob. I doubt she'll make one thousand times lightspeed."*

The ship was, it was true, in a shabby state. As well as painting over the emblems of the ship's previous owners, the USZ refitters also seemed to have tried to paint over micrometeoroid scars and long streaks of corrosion; seen from close up, the ship was a mess of welds and repairs.

Cleo leaned over to the console. "This is, erm, Mick Korolev. Our pilot is injured, and we are incapable of movement, over."

There was a pause, after which the console said, not without suspicion:

"You speak very good English for a Russian, Mikoyan-Korolev, over."

Cleo frowned. "I lyearn Yinglish vyery well in Byeautiful Soviet KGB", she replied. "Syize of an Yelephant", she added.

"Можем мы помочьвам, over?"

"Ah, repyeat plyease, byeautiful Soviet radio is nyot fyunctionying", improvised Cleo. "Is dyamyaged in myeteor stryike that yis also damagying pilot."

There was another pause.

*"Don't you mean meteor*oid, *Mikoyan-Korolev, over?"* said the radio.

"Meteors is meteoroids outside planetary atmospheres", whispered Glenn Bob helpfully through the console speaker. *"Don't go askin me why now."*

"It's a bit of a crowded house over there by the sound of things", said the voice from the cruiser. *"Do Americans often travel on Russian military vessels, over?"*

"Shucks and fudge", said Glenn Bob. *"I plumb forgot there they could hear me iffen I talked into the radio. Aw dang, I forgot I done talked into the radio again."*

"You certainly did", said the radio. *"Prepare for docking, over."*

"Uh, I don't think we got us no airlock nor docking clamps", said Glenn Bob, and added, *"Over."*

"We syeek asylum in Dyemocratic Yunited Styates of Zodiac", added Cleo.

"That's the spirit. Can you make a space walk across to this vessel at all, over?"

"Aw, we don't got us no space suits neither over."

The next pause was very, very long. Then, the radio said:

"You're flying a high performance fighter without a space suit?"

"That's a positive", replied Glenn Bob.

"There aren't many suits in our size", said Ant.

"How old are you exactly, Mikoyan-Korolev?"

"Twelve", said Cleo.

"Twelve", said Ant. "And a half", he added.

"Twelve point six", said Glenn Bob.

"Don't move. And don't touch anything. *We're going to try and take you into our lifeboat bay."* There was a sound of muffled conversation from the radio, one side of which went like this:

"What d'you mean, it's blocked with essential supplies?"

"I don't call that essential."

"I don't care how many households on Gondolin have to do without soft toilet paper, Mr. Ruskin. Lives are at stake here. If it's not needed, kick it out of the airlock."

16 - Fantasm

The *Jervis Bay*'s lifeboats were tiny saucers even smaller than Mr. Turpin's had been, and they had had to do an elaborate dance to allow the fighter to be gently nudged and towed into the cruiser's boat dock. The boat dock was small and cramped, only slightly wider than the fighter, and lifeboats, towing cables and men in patched and threadbare space suits had all been needed to squeeze the vessel in.

"We're going to need to pressurise the boat bay before we can get you out of your vehicle", said the voice in the console. *"Hang on and don't throw open your canopy just yet."*

The boat dock doors whined shut, and a gentle hissing sounded from the walls. Most of the cockpit glass was misted up with Ant and Cleo's breath, but Ant could just make out a dial on the wall outside with a needle wobbling from zero up towards one thousand. When the needle reached one thousand, the voice from the cruiser said:

"All right, you can pile out now. Be careful, though, there's one half gee of gravity in here, we're under thrust."

Ant punched out the canopy release gratefully, and tumbled out of the cockpit clean through the saucer's wing, gasping for air. Cleo and Glenn Bob followed, Cleo kissing the steel as if it was holy ground.

"Oh, sweet English-speaking noncommunist deck", said Cleo. "I will never again leave you."

"Hmm", said a voice. "It looks as if your oxygen recycler packed up. Bally good show we found you when we did."

Ant looked up. He saw a pair of boots in military trousers, and a gleaming metal cane. Someone had pressed the trousers until hairs could be split on the creases. The voice speaking from above the trousers was the same one Ant had heard over the radio.

Then the man behind the trousers crouched down to look under the wing, putting his weight on his cane to do so, and Ant was able to see the top half of him for the first time. He was about the size of Ant's father, but older, with an entirely white head of hair. He was wearing a tunic in the same blue-grey as his trousers, and was flanked by men wearing uniforms that looked similar, but less important. The less important men were carrying rocket rifles. However, this was not so bad. Ant was getting used to rocket rifles by now.

The important man tipped his cap at Ant. He took a pipe from the corner of his mouth.

"Permission to come aboard, Captain?" he said.

Ant looked across at Glenn Bob grudgingly. "He's the Captain", he said. "He flew the ship."

The man saluted to Glenn Bob. "Pleased to make your acquaintance, Captain", he said. "Star Commodore Bentley Drummond, commander of the *Jervis Bay*, at your service."

Glenn Bob saluted back. "Right pleased to meet you", he said, as if he didn't mean it.

"And this will be the young Russian lady", said the Star Commodore.

"Erm", said Cleo. "I'm not really Russian. My family come from St. Lucia", she said, as if this was a consolation. She curtseyed politely. Commodore Drummond bowed gravely in return.

Then, he straightened suddenly as something oozed around his trouser bottoms. He looked down, and twenty-four varicoloured eyestalks stared back up at him. Truman J. Slughound had somehow slithered silently off the fighter and coiled himself around the Commodore's ankles. The Commodore's bodyguard jerked into action, and the sluggie was looking down the barrels of several rocket rifles in under a second.

"Erm", said the Commodore. "Does he bite?"

"Not unless you're made of polypropylene", said Cleo, giggling.

"It's OK, he seems to like you", said Glenn Bob. "For some reason."

Commodore Drummond's cheeks drained of colour. He stared down at the excited sluggie in horror. "Please", he said, his face ashen, "please remove it."

Glenn Bob came forward and whistled. "Bad sluggie! Bad, bad sluggie! Here boy, there!"

Truman J. Slughound unwound from the Commodore and propelled himself in the direction of Glenn Bob. The Commodore inspected his legs as if to check they were still all there, then hobbled forward on his cane and ran his eyes along the Russian saucer.

"Golly", he said. "Gosh", he added.

"*He's looking at it as if he fancies it*", whispered Ant to Cleo.

"Oh, I do, I do", said the Commodore without a trace of embarrassment. "So this is what a *Fantasm* looks like close up, is it?"

"Fantasm?" said Ant.

"We call them Fantasms. The Red Star Fleet calls them Mikoyan-Korolev 1000's. The only reports we've had of them so far have been as blips on long range radar. Usually the target doesn't live long enough to report anything closer. Our boffins are going to *love* taking this crate to pieces." He squinted at the pilot's cockpit, which was misted over. "I say, is there still someone in there?"

Ant peered after him. "Oh yes", he said. "Mr. Turpin."

"*Richard* Turpin? *Lieutenant* Richard Turpin? The *Highwayman?*" The Commodore lost all his cool immediately. "Of course, I should have known if anyone would bring in a *Fantasm* it'd be Turpin. Outstanding man, Turpin. Is there any way to open this bubble from the outside?" He walked forward as if about to stoop under the saucer, then seemed to think better of it and turned and snapped at his subordinates. "Mr. Starkey, get a squad of men with cutting gear and a first aid team down here at the double before he dies of CO2 poisoning."

He stepped back from under the saucer, took out a monogrammed handkerchief, and mopped his brow. "We're close to our destination", he said. "Please follow me. You'll need to be strapped in for the final descent through the atmosphere." He turned and swaggered off, leaning on his stick heavily. A door squealed open automatically to let him pass.

The soldiers motioned (with their eyes rather than their rifles, a detail that Ant found encouraging) for Ant, Cleo, Glenn Bob and Truman J. Slughound to follow. One of the soldiers leaned down close to Ant's ear, and whispered:

"By the way - the Commodore lost 'is left and right legs in an accident. *Both* 'is legs is polypropylene."

***

Ant fell into step beside the Commodore. "Excuse me, sir", he said, raising a hand politely. "Did I hear you mention 'Gondolin' on the radio a few minutes ago?"

"You did indeed, and you're all about to visit it."

Glenn Bob pursed his lips, gnashed his teeth and set his jaw. It looked painful. "Sir, I must caution you that, as a loyal citizen of the United States of America's Colonies in Space, I would feel myself duty bound to report the location of Gondolin should I discover it."

The Commodore smiled at Glenn Bob. "Ah, so you're USA, not US Zee, are you? We'll just have to make sure you don't go anywhere near a navigation chart, then, Captain."

"I must add, sir, that in view of your gallant rescue of myself and my comrades, I would consider it a dishonourable act to try and discover the location of Gondolin there, sir. I only mean to draw your attention to the fact that I would feel duty bound to report Gondolin's location was I to discover it accidentally."

At all of this, the Commodore's eyes narrowed. "You're from New Dixie, aren't you, Captain?"

Glenn Bob stuck his chest out proudly. "I am indeed, sir."

"Then I take it you haven't heard the, ah...news."

Glenn Bob bit his lip. Cleo answered for him.

"We were there, sir", she said.

"Indeed?" The Commodore raised an eyebrow as he stopped to rattle the door of a compartment labelled MEDICINAL ALCOHOL STORE to check whether it was locked. "Then I take it you know it wasn't us."

"No", said Glenn Bob, fixing the Commodore with a stainless steel glare, "we don't."

"We weren't at the colony when it was, um, attacked", said Ant. "That's how we survived, I imagine."

"It must have been terrible for ones so young", said the Commodore. "Any idea of the ratio of casualties to survivors, by any chance?"

"There were *no* casualties", said Glenn Bob firmly. "My mom and dad are still alive."

"Back up there a moment", said the Captain. "How can there have been an attack without casualties?"

"There were no *bodies*", said Ant helpfully.

"So", reasoned the Commodore slowly, "whoever was responsible for the attack was interested in taking the bodies. Whether those bodies were dead or alive."

"Alive", said Glenn Bob defiantly.

"Quite, quite", agreed the Commodore. "It was a Soviet attack, of course", he added, signing a sheaf of forms a crewman had run up to him with. "It was a Soviet ship that relayed the message that the colony had been attacked. Too much of a coincidence that a Soviet ship *just happened to be in the area*, you see."

"No", said Ant, shaking his head firmly. "It wasn't the Soviets."

"Then who?" said the Commodore. "Aliens?" Ant could tell that answering 'yes' would be a mistake.

"Who made the ship the Americans found crashed at Roswell?" said Cleo.

"We don't know", said the Commodore, heaving himself up a set of steps to a higher deck and grimacing as he did so, "that they found any such vessel. The United States of America tell us they found a crashed ship at Roswell, the Russians say they found one at Tunguska, and both say the other side copied their designs. To be quite honest, we don't know who to believe - if anybody! If either of them can convince us the science behind the saucer drives is alien, you see, we're less likely to try to understand it ourselves." He stopped, leaned over a tiny grille on the wall, and puffed into it with his pipe. Alarms sounded deafeningly all the way through the ship. "Smoke detectors working splendidly, Bo'sun", beamed the Commodore. "Well *done*."

Ant was contemptuous. "You mean you don't know what makes your own engines work?"

A crewman, who Ant assumed was the Bo'sun, pelted back down the corridor yelling "NO FIRE! NO FIRE! FALSE ALARM! FALSE ALARM!"

The Commodore looked after the Bo'sun. "Capital fellow, the Bo'sun", he said. Then, he shrugged. "The Americans give us blueprints, and we copy them. Sometimes we...muck about with them a bit, and see what happens. But no - we don't really understand what makes them go. Nor do the Americans either, I think, for what it's worth."

"But I thought this was a USZ ship", said Cleo.

"Certainly it is. But it's a USZ ship *from Gondolin*. Gondolin's the thirteenth star, the thirteenth colony of the United States of the Zodiac. And each State of the Zodiac is an independent planet, and twelve of them are American, and we, as you've no doubt noticed, are British. The others are very suspicious of us." He tapped Ant and Cleo on the shoulders. "And don't think I haven't noticed *you* two are Britishers, too. You'll be from Her Majesty's Colony on Lalande 21185, I take it."

Ant blinked. "Erm - no", he said. "Northampton."

The Commodore blinked back. He removed his pipe from his mouth.

"You're from *Earth?*", he said. "Oh, my dear, dear fellows. How confused you must be!"

Then a pair of double doors opened in front of them, and Ant saw stars.

The bridge of the *Jervis Bay* opened on to space. The stars outside slithered across the windows in a way that suggested the glass they were being seen through was thicker than the glass in the average learners' swimming pool.

"CAPTAIN ON THE BRIDGE!" squawked someone, causing the entire room to snap to attention, though it seemed they had been concentrating fairly fiercely even before the Commodore had come in.

"Cease deceleration burn and bring her head round", he said. "Close heatshields."

There was a chorus of Aye sir's, and the Commodore motioned to Glenn Bob, Ant and Cleo to hold on to handles on the walls. A red light winked on saying GRAVITY LOSS, accompanied by a klaxon. Crewmen who weren't in their seats scurried to them.

Ant felt the jumping-into-water feeling of the ship closing down thrust. He had to hold on hard to the handles to stop his feet floating free of the deck. As the ship turned, the stars in the windows went out. Something bigger and far fiercer-burning was filling the sky - a nearby sun. Huge steel shutters began closing over the bridge windows.

"*I don't recognise none o'they stars*", whispered Glenn Bob to Ant. "*We're a powerful long way from home.*"

Remembering that the Commodore had said 'heatshield', Ant asked: "Are we travelling down through a planetary atmosphere now, sir?"

Loud bangs sounded from the other side of the shutters. "Half the atmosphere's made of lumps of flying rock at this height", muttered a crewman.

The Commodore, meanwhile, seemed delighted that Ant had figured this out. "Why, yes. Most small ships, and some big ones, can land purely under their own steam, but big old lumbertubs like this one still need a little help from atmospheric friction, I'm afraid. Rather like your Earth 'Space Shuttles'. Danged dangerous contraptions to my mind. Sitting on a bally great firework, all the way up into orbit? No, give me a poorly understood mysterious alien propulsion system any day."

A crewman at the console cleared his throat loudly. "Ahem. We're through the outer atmosphere, sir."

"Very good. Open the shutters."

The heatshields wheezed back from the windows, and a few final chunks of airborne cinder bounced off the glass. There was a planet outside.

Gondolin, if this *was* Gondolin, was a world that looked as if it had been made with a pastrycutter. Circular seas, circular mountain ranges, circular island chains, plateaux and, in places, worrying lakes of fire covered the place from pole to pole, making it look as if someone had taken a map of the Moon and spilt water into its dry seas, making them real.

"What you see here, of course, is a heavily meteorited landscape", informed the Commodore, "formed by the erosive and depositive action of a Phobos-sized asteroid or two crashing into Gondolin once every few days or so." And as Ant watched, one did. Halfway round the planet, a searing white trail scuttled across his retinas and impacted into the landscape with a blaze of light. A ring of fire streaked out from the point of detonation, spreading out hundreds, maybe even thousands of kilometres. Ant felt sure that nothing beneath that glowing wave could live.

"As you can imagine", said the Commodore, "native life on Gondolin hasn't progressed beyond a primitive stage".

The ship was skimming above a wildly cratered landscape. Parts of it steamed like newly laid road tar, parts of it were piles of lifeless stone, but some parts were a patchwork of sky blue, sea green, sulphur yellow, blood red and deep violet.

"That's grass down there!" said Cleo. "It's green!"

"And water!" said Ant.

"It looks like a real, living planet, I'll grant you", said Mr. Starkey, staring at the landscape angrily, "but it's all lichen. A fingernail's thickness of lichen, over solid rock!"

"Mr. Starkey is correct", said Commodore Drummond. "The first explorers to crash land here had run out of drinking water, and their spectrometer told them there was fresh liquid water at the planetary equator. Unfortunately, the native species of lichen *Instaraquae Saxiphagia* reflects light in almost the exact same spectrum as pure standing water, and it grows only in desert regions."

"Did they die?" said Cleo, wide-eyed.

"They did not", said the Commodore haughtily. "One of them was Flight Sergeant Ronald Turpin of His Majesty's Royal Space Force. The others were Leading Aircraftman Winston Pink, Senior Aircraftman Bahadar Singh, and Flight Lieutenant Arthur Wellesley Drummond - who was, as it happens, my father. They survived by centrifuging the sweat from their own long underwear, and on such heroic endeavour is our colony of Gondolin built."

Cleo narrowed her eyes. "But you have proper supplies of drinking water now, yes?"

"Of course. All modern conveniences." The Commodore swelled with pride. "Why, in the Civic Hall, we even have a single flushing toilet. And we make our own soap. Out of lichen."

Ant and Cleo exchanged glances. This was not good.

The saucer was dropping down into the shadow of a range of ragged-peaked mountains, in the centre of which was a circle of brilliant emerald.

"Lichen", said Cleo.

But as the saucer settled down slowly on the gentlest whiff of power, the green was revealed to be grass, stretching away over rolling plains like a gentle dusting of down. There was a barely perceptible bump as the landing struts kissed the grass blades.

"We are on the green, sir", announced Mr. Starkey.

"Hole in one, Mr. Starkey", said the Commodore. "Now, Captain, if you and your crew will do us the honour of accompanying me, I'll show you around Gondolin."

17 - Sheer Neurally-Induced Ecstasy

"Northampton, eh?" said the Commodore. "Stopped in the station once at Northampton." He scratched his head with his stick. "Was about five at the time, I think. Mama got off at the wrong station. Terrible coffee."

"You lived on Earth?" said Ant.

They were walking across a flower meadow as lush and green as any in England. Behind them, the acre or so of steel on the hull of the cruiser cracked and creaked as the metal cooled.

"This type of grass", said the Commodore, "reflects light of the exact same spectrum as a native type of lichen, *Smaragda*. Anyone looking for a patch of grass with a telescope from orbit would find a great deal of lichen. Yes", he said, strolling away in the direction of a featureless grassy knoll, "I did live on Earth for quite a while. Nice place. Those Beatles fellows, are they still together? 'Can't Buy Me Loooooove, Ah, Everybody Tells Me So, Give Me Mooooooney, That's What I Want'?"

"Erm, not quite together", said Ant.

"One dead, two alive, one a vegetarian on the Mull of Kintyre", said Cleo.

"Gosh", said the Commodore. "As bad as that?"

He tapped the side of the knoll three times in quick succession with his cane. Nothing happened. Impatiently, he tapped it again.

"*Is something supposed to happen?*" whispered Glenn Bob to Ant. Ant shrugged.

Then, a perfect circle of green at the centre of the mound lifted from the grass around it and began to rotate upwards, as if unscrewing. After a few moments' rotation, it came away entirely and rolled away into the grass. Beneath it, a man's head, in USZ uniform, popped out. It saluted.

The man, however, was not as other men. His hair grew in a peculiar fashion, long at the back and short on top.

"*Look at that hair*", said Ant, nudging Cleo. "*Do you think he's some sort of alien?*"

"It's a mullet, Ant", said Cleo sourly. "Your father probably had one in about 1982."

"Good morning sir", said the man.

The Commodore returned the salute grumpily. "Look lively, Falconer. Get her clothes on before an enemy vessel spots her in the buff."

Falconer saluted again and disappeared. The Commodore turned round to look at the Jervis Bay.

"Splendid fellow, Falconer", he said. "Wouldn't be without him. Here they come! They'll have the old girl under wraps before you can say Perihelion."

As Ant and Cleo followed the Commodore's eyes, every one of the small green knolls around the cruiser rotated open. Ground crew in USZ uniforms scrambled out of grassy hatchways, running up to the cruiser, attaching hoses and lines to the hull, inspecting meteoroid holes with disapproving clucks. Many of them were dragging rolls of what looked like canvas. When the rolls were spread out, however, they seemed to disappear into the grass they were being rolled across. Ant stared at a nearby roll until his eyes hurt and he realised that it was made of bright green astroturf, exactly the same colour as the grass. Hoisted over the cruiser on wires and armatures, the fabric soon covered it so completely that it was difficult to believe a warship as big as a medium-sized town hall had ever been there.

"Splendid", beamed the Commodore, like a kindly headmaster on School Prize Day.

"I like what you've done with your planet", said Cleo.

"Thank you", said the Commodore. "Most kind." He gestured with his stick. "Over there you can see our orchard. Erm, not strictly an *apple* orchard, I'm afraid. Apple trees only produce knee-high weeds in a Gondolin climate. But for some reason, lichees grow to gigantic size. Erm, whether we want them to or not."

"Terrific!" Cleo clapped her hands. "I *love* lichees!"

At the mention of enjoying eating lichees, the Commodore ground his teeth together and said nothing. The lichee orchard, clearly visible now they had come to the top of the grass rise, was a confused jungle of massive green leaves and fist-sized spiky fruit.

"They, ah, grow a little *larger* in the low gravity", said the Commodore. "We've had to cover them with camouflage sheeting so they can't be seen from orbit." Ant could see a flimsy, astroturf-coloured set of awnings secured to the tops of the trees by guyropes.

Cleo, meanwhile, was running down the lea side of the hill towards the orchard.

"AH - DON'T PICK ONE", called the Commodore. "YOU COULD GET YOURSELF STUNG QUITE BADLY."

Cleo stopped dead. "How so?" she said weakly.

The Commodore sauntered casually down the rise, holding the small of his back as he did so. When he eventually reached the bottom, he raised his cane and parted the leaves of one of the nearby lichees.

"Because *they* grow to enormous size here as well", he said.

The Commodore had revealed a gigantic stinging nettle leaf the size of a coffee table. Each spine on the back of the horrible thing was the length and thickness of a darning needle.

"There's enough acetylcholine in one of these spines to kill a big cat, a puppy dog, or a human baby", he said, frowning. "Never blunder around here in the dark. We grow them all around our perimeter, too, to keep the colony safe."

"Safe from *what*?" said Ant. "Dinosaurs?"

"We've only explored a tiny part of Gondolin", shrugged the Commodore. "So far the only native life we've found has been little more complex than bacteria, but there could very well *be* dinosaurs out there for all we know." He let the lichee leaves fall back over the nettle. "They make excellent soup, too, you know, boiled down. We supplement this with fungus and the occasional experimental piece of native lichen. Erm, the native lichen is still *very* much experimental at this juncture, I'm afraid."

"Gosh", said Cleo. "Does this mean you live an idyllic vegetarian existence?"

The Commodore blinked. "Pardon me? Oh, good gracious no. Perish the thought. Here, let me show you where we kill the pigs."

Cleo's face went purple.

"Don't worry", said the Commodore, patting her arm reassuringly. "It's a wonderfully safe and humane process. I believe there is nothing like it on Earth." He raised his stick and pointed further round the trees.

The only reason why Ant had failed to notice the pigs was that he had assumed they were large flabby pink boulders of some description. Besides being pink and flabby, they also looked extremely contented. Although the muck they were rolling in was a deep blue green and resembled oil paint rather than mud, this did not seem to bother them. Some of them were even rooting in it with their snouts. One of them leapt up onto the fence that separated them from Ant, Cleo and Glenn Bob, and grunted happily at the Commodore.

Suddenly, a keening mechanical note sounded. The pigs appeared to take no notice.

"Aha!" said the Commodore. "The siren. We are in luck. They are going to kill one now. We must stay very still, and go no closer. Watch."

Ant and Cleo, Cleo with a visible lump in her throat, watched as the pigs continued to roll, root and grunt.

"Now, keep your eye on the porker in that far corner", said the Commodore. "He's the closest to the Machine."

The pig in question was rummaging happily in a pile of earth, apparently oblivious of how Close To The Machine it was. Ant unhappily reminded himself that he had no more idea where the Machine was than the pig did.

The Commodore appeared to sense his discomfort, and pointed. "Over there. See?"

At the end of the Commodore's cane, Ant picked out an oddly-shaped aerial poking from a clump of what he now realised was rather obvious plastic foliage at the edge of the pigs' corral. The clump, he noticed, also appeared to be moving; and natural clumps of vegetation, he reminded himself, seldom had exhaust pipes and caterpillar tracks.

"They disguise the projector", said the Commodore, watching Ant's eyes. "Makes the piggies happier with it, you see."

Suddenly, another sound - almost deafeningly loud, but only at the very edges of hearing - filled the air. It sounded to Ant like a television turned on but with the sound turned down. Leaves vibrated on the trees despite the almost total silence, and the air itself seemed electric, as if at the onset of a storm.

The aerial flared bright green and purple for the blink of an eye - so brightly that the trees and bushes cast a shadow from it - and Ant felt a definite warm glow wash over him. What did it matter, he thought, that he was a squillion light years from home, that he had been in danger of death for weeks, that his joints hurt and his stomach ached and his entire body was crying out for sleep, food and warmth in any order they became available. How could it be a problem that his Mum and Dad had no idea where he was, and were probably already blaming each other for stealing him off each other? If they could only experience this feeling, this marvellous, wonderful feeling, they would not have a care in the world. They would not care at all, *he* would not care at all, if he took a rocket pistol and unloaded a full clip into his forehead, and would laugh while he did it.

Over in the corner of the corral, the pig flopped over on its back with a beatific porcine smile, raising all four trotters in the air.

Ant shook himself. The universe came back to normal. The pig's feet, however, were still pointing at the sky. A dandelion seed settled inside one of the pig's nostrils. The pig did not move.

"Marvellously humane device", said the Commodore. "Died of sheer neurally induced ecstasy, don't you know."

"That", said Ant, "is *horrible.*" Despite the fact that it was horrible, however, he was having difficulty wiping the smile off his face.

The Commodore, however, appeared not to hear. "The animal, you see, has its nerve endings affected by a powerful ultrasonic pulse at a set of precisely determined frequencies. Dies of happiness. Invented by two of our chaps, Gould and Dawkins. Splendid chaps." He waved at two men who were standing in the next field over holding remote controls. They waved back.

Commodore Drummond strolled over to the fence and poked the dead porker with his stick through the bars. "What a way to go, eh?"

"And of course", said Cleo sweetly, "think of the military applications."

The Commodore turned round and squinted at Cleo in puzzlement. "What? *Military*, did you say?"

"Of course. Why", she said, appearing to think deeply on the subject, "if a planet of, say, Soviets or Americans doesn't do what you say, you need simply position a giant one of these in orbit way above them and *turn it on.*"

The Commodore looked at Cleo in alarm. "But, ah, that would be *murder.*"

"No, surely not", said Cleo, smiling beautifully. "After all, they'd die of *happiness.*"

"You're one of these Vegetarians, aren't you", said the Commodore, staring at her in deep suspicion.

"I apologise to my lettuce before I eat it", said Cleo.

"It's true", said Ant, still grinning insanely. "She does."

"Well", said the Commodore tartly, we do have a few of *your sort* here." He waved his stick back towards the *Jervis Bay*. "Richard Turpin, for example."

"See, Cleo", grinned Ant. "Mr. Turpin can't be all bad. He's a vegetarian, like you."

"*Hitler*", said Cleo emphatically, "was a vegetarian."

"SESAME", proclaimed the Commodore, raising his hand on high like Moses parting the waters. The grassy bank in front of them swung up on hinges, and wheezed up into the air on struts, dropping clods of earth. Behind the bank, a tunnel, lit by long lines of lights, led into the hillside.

The Commodore hurried through and waited until Ant and Cleo followed, then tapped the tunnel wall twice with his cane. Arthritically, the tunnel door rumbled shut behind them. "Can't be too careful", he said. "Not born in a barn, enemy always watching and so forth." He appeared to be walking a little more slowly now, but still kept pointing proudly to the various features of his domain as they strolled through it.

"See that? That's what we call an *electric light*. Do you have those on Earth? Oh, silly me, of course you do."

The passage crossed others going back and forth inside the hill. The other passages were busy. People passed wheeling handcarts loaded with hoses, cables, tools and mysterious pieces of equipment in the direction of the *Jervis Bay*. All of them, men and women alike, saluted the Commodore.

One of them was dressed in a jumpsuit and carried a flight helmet. However, what most interested Ant about her was the fact that she was a she, taller than the Commodore, with her head shaved close to her scalp. Despite this, she was also so strikingly beautiful it hurt Ant's eyes to look at her.

"Where's Turpin with that Moke? I heard he'd come in."

"Mr. Turpin", said the Commodore, "came in *injured,* Lieutenant. And the Moke is lost."

"That *idiot!*" spat the Lieutenant. "Some day he's going to get us all killed! Erm, he isn't *badly* injured, is he?"

The Commodore shook his head. "And he appears to have exchanged the Moke for a Soviet Fantasm fighter which you might want to take a look at. It's in the *Jervis*'s lifeboat bay right now."

The Lieutenant's eyes went wide. Ant had seen such looks on the faces of children who'd been told there was a new bicycle in the garage.

"Off you go, Lieutenant", said the Commodore.

The Lieutenant almost skipped away down the corridor. Before she left, however, her eyes lit on Ant, Glenn Bob and Cleo.

"What are *these*?" she said.

"Waifs and strays", smiled the Commodore. "*This* fellow", he said, clapping Glenn Bob on the shoulder, "was piloting the Fantasm when it was brought in."

The Lieutenant looked at Glenn Bob with evident surprise. Ant could tell she was impressed. "Russian?"

"I", said Glenn Bob, "am one hundred per cent American."

"I am confused", said the Lieutenant. "Are these Americans too?"

"I'm afraid Richard appears to have managed to abduct them at some point", said the Commodore. "It's really all quite embarrassing. I've no doubt that he judged his mission to be compromised in some way, and that's why he took them on board, but..." the Commodore suddenly paused as if he'd thought of something truly horrible, leaned down to Ant, and said quietly: "...ah...he didn't use you as *hostages*, did he?"

Cleo's mouth worked soundlessly on new things to call Turpin, but evidently could find nothing bad enough. "I never thought of that!"

"No, he *didn't*", said Ant firmly. "He was wounded in the hand when we met him. He only needed us to load up cargo and operate the controls."

"It figures", grinned the Lieutenant. "Turpin needs three hands to pilot a saucer most days of the week."

"Ahem, that's not strictly true", interrupted the Commodore. "Mr. Turpin is in fact an excellent pilot. It's simply that Lieutenant Farthing here believes herself to be a better one."

"Quite true", said Lieutenant Farthing.

"We're English", said Cleo. "From Earth."

The Lieutenant put out a hand. "Penelope Farthing at your service", she said. "I'm English from Outer Space." Her gaze strayed from Cleo to Ant. "Ah. I see *this* one has already met Messrs. Gould and Dawkins."

"Erm, yes", said the Commodore. "We have been showing them the Humane Killer."

"I thought so", nodded the Lieutenant. "That's Gould and Dawkins for you. Wonderful at target acquisition systems and laser-guided munitions, terrible at domestic plumbing." She put out a hand and tweaked Ant hard on the nose. Ant's lockjaw smile magically disappeared.

"Ow", said Ant. "Thanks...I think."

"Don't mention it", said Lieutenant Farthing. "The face muscles go into spasm, you see. *Jervis Bay*'s boat deck, did you say, sir?"

"The very same", nodded the Commodore.

The Lieutenant saluted and jogged off down the corridor.

"It is no doubt apparent", said the Commodore wanly, "that certain of my junior officers salute me only when they are minded to do so."

"Why don't you have them keelhauled or something", said Ant.

"Can't afford to. Need all the men and women I have."

He set off down the corridor, head heavy, leaning hard on his cane, towards a large set of steel doors marked LIVING QUARTERS! PLEASE WIPE YOUR FEET! LEAVE RADIOACTIVITY OUTSIDE!

The Commodore sank himself down onto a rough seat cut into the rock next to the door, and struggled with his knees until both of his feet popped off. Once they were off, he sat back, the empty bottoms of his trousers drooping down the wall, sighed hugely, and mopped his brow with a handkerchief.

Then, he winked at Ant and Cleo, leaned down to the floor, picked up a manky-looking doormat, picked up his feet one by one, and wiped them carefully. Then, he carefully clicked his feet back onto his knees, rose unsteadily onto his feet, and walked on into Gondolin.

Beyond the door, Gondolin was a city.

18 - A School of Mullets

Men in uniform were dashing about here and there, so it did still look a little like a military base, but there were also people in what looked like a poor attempt at civilian clothing. Men were wearing shirts that had plainly been military at some point in their existences, but which had been dyed, had their sleeves cut short, and had DE LA MAISON DE CHEZ MADAME MICHELLE, GONDOLIN sewn onto the pockets. There were occasional pieces of Earth clothing, worn proudly. Cleo saw a girl in a KIDS FROM FAME T-shirt, and another in a faded parka which read !!!ACIIIIIID!!!

"These people", said Cleo as they followed the Commodore through a cramped corridor, "are in need of about one hundred good haircuts."

"Too many military buzz cuts", agreed Ant.

"It is not", said Cleo, "the military buzz cuts I mind. It is the attempts at fashion I find most disturbing. Somewhere in this benighted anthill is a barber who learned how to do the Farrah Flick from a TV signal transmitted in 1979 and liked it so much he did free ones for all his friends and neighbours. *Even"*, she stressed, in a quivering voice, *"the men."*

"What's a Farrah Flick?" said Ant.

They came out in a chamber which, by Gondolin standards, was huge - at least the size of a normal comprehensive classroom - and filled with maps, charts, and black-and-white silhouettes of saucer-shaped space vessels labelled KNOW YOUR ENEMY. Oil paintings also lined the room, though Ant imagined it must be difficult to attach them to the over-arching walls. There was a painting of the *Jervis Bay,* looking rather shinier than she did in real life, and for some reason, opposite it, a picture of a warship at sea, firing guns. In a dark corner of the ceiling, among a number of paintings of men in full dress uniform, was a picture of Commodore Drummond in full dress uniform. Underneath this picture was a photograph of a rather younger man shaking hands with a grumpy-looking lady in a Marks & Spencer's dress.

"Welcome", said the Commodore, "to my office. We'll try and make this debriefing as informal as possible."

He sank into a chair with a weary sigh, reached down to his knees, and, completely without embarrassment, began unscrewing his legs again. Ant didn't like to pry into what the ends of his thighs looked like. Once he'd unfastened both his legs, which looked like what Ant had always imagined a robot's legs should look like, he threw them into a corner, where they rattled straight into an umbrella stand which already contained several pointing sticks and dismantled rocket rifles.

"SHOT!" cried the Commodore, and raised his fist in the air victoriously. His eyes twinkled as he produced a cardboard box from a desk drawer. "Anyone for a Dairylea Slice?"

"Yeuch", said Ant with feeling.

"Oh dear", said the Commodore. "I always keep a box of these in my desk. Mr. Turpin informs me that they are very popular on Earth. '*Kids will do anything for a Dairylea Slice*' were, I believe, his exact words. Capital fellow, Turpin."

"Mr. Turpin", said Ant, "has been watching too much television advertising."

"Kids", said Cleo, "will do a great deal to *avoid* a Dairylea Slice."

"Oh dear", said the Commodore, sounding quite upset. "Ah well. Be that as it may - allow me to introduce Captain Ben Yancy, our liaison with the Zodiac Fleet."

The chamber also contained a man of the Commodore's age, dressed in a similar uniform, though one that looked a bit better turned out, and cut from cloth of a slightly different colour. The man's hair was greying, though his shoulders were still thick as a bricklayer's, and his neck was disconcertingly wider than his head.

Far more interestingly, though, he was black.

"Obviously Gondolin doesn't have enough of a fleet yet to be able to contribute to the cut and thrust of operations", said Commodore Drummond, "but we hope to pull our weight in time."

"Honoured to meet you all", said Captain Yancy, who appeared to be an American as well as being black.

Glenn Bob stared at Yancy in horror. "They done made a negro a *Captain*?"

"I'm from King", said the Captain. "Our world was first colonized in 1967, using Vietnam veterans reported Missing In Action. It's 95 per cent black. Originally I believe the plan was to call the planet Nixon, but after the revolution -"

"Rebellion", corrected Glenn Bob.

Ant saw the Commodore mouth 'New Dixie' at the Captain. Captain Yancy mouthed a silent 'oh' back, nodded, and shut up, staring hard at Glenn Bob. Glenn Bob stared hard back.

"Now", said the Commodore. "As I promised, I suppose I'd better explain how British and American people come to be in space."

"We've already heard the USA version", said Ant.

"But we've heard their version of the Second World War too", said Cleo. "And that stinks."

The Commodore and Captain exchanged grins.

"Well", said the Commodore, "the US Zed version is as follows. The United States of America originally discovers Saucer Drive in the late nineteen forties. No-one else knows they have it. They plant colonies in thirteen star systems before Communist sympathizers hand over blueprints of the Astromoke Mark 1, America's first mass-produced spacecraft, to Soviet Russia."

"The Soviets are are dismayed", continued the Captain. "Don't forget, they've just spent enough roubles on their space programme to pay God's wages; and they don't even *believe* in God. They put everything they have into saucer research - don't do much new in rocketry for the next ten years. After a little while, US saucer pilots start seeing other vessels on their long range sensors - ships that reply to radio hailing in Russian."

"Meanwhile", said the Commodore, "the British Secret Service are dismayed to discover that one of their country's diplomats, a man called George Blake, is a Russian spy. They are doubly dischuffed when he tells them that their Russian Cold War enemies know more about a top secret American space exploration programme than they do."

"The British Prime Minister of the time, Harold Macmillan, threatens to go public with the whole thing and use it as an excuse to pull out of NATO", said the Captain. "The Americans have no choice but to hand over a working Astromoke Mark 1 to the British too. Soon the Brits have their own little colony orbiting Lalande 21185, a snug little place where the daytime temperatures reach one hundred Celsius and it occasionally rains sulphuric acid."

"They transfer a small boy who was quite happy at his toys at Winchester College to a set of ceramic-tiled bunkers underground 8.1 light years away", said the Commodore sadly. "Rather like an enormous Gents', it was."

"And a few years after that", said the Captain, "they transfer another small boy from a military college in Virginia to a new school somewhere in Canis where you can't play hookey to see a movie unless you're prepared to steal a starship; and no-one is allowed outside to play, because there is no *air* outside."

"Surely you were allowed *some* movies?" said Ant. Somehow, it was the lack of movies that disturbed him more than the lack of air.

"We were", said the Captain grimly. "*John Wayne* movies."

Ant fell silent, appalled.

"So how did the British and American colonies come to revolt, sir?" said Cleo.

The Captain and Commodore exchanged glances. The Commodore nodded to the Captain.

"We have to wind time backwards slightly here. In 1960", said the Captain, "a new President of the USA was elected. His name was John F. Kennedy, and you may have heard of him. Although he actually increased defence spending during his time in office, he was what Americans call a 'Democrat', a sort of natural enemy of the military. He was also the first Democrat to be president for eight years. The military didn't trust him - eventually, as you probably know, they had him assassinated. They *certainly* didn't trust him enough to tell him flying saucers had existed for ten years and were crewed by Americans."

"That was when it started", said the Commodore. "From that time on, no American president has known. Only a handful of people Americans call 'five star generals' and 'chiefs of intelligence' have been in on the secret. Things seem to have been similar in Russia - our best information indicates that Andropov was the last Premier to know anything about Soviet Russia's colonies in space. Hence Russia's colonies in space are *still* Soviet."

"Then a thing happened", said the Captain, "called 'The Vietnam War'".

"I know about that", interrupted Ant.

"Sylvester Stallone and Mr. T. were in it", agreed Cleo.

"The Americans won it", said Ant. "With their shirts off, for the most part."

Captain Yancy and Commodore Drummond exchanged confused glances.

"Our information was rather different", said the Commodore. "In any case, the American military felt, as the Vietnam War ended, that it was feared and distrusted by many of the citizens who were supposed to be grateful for its protection."

"Right about that time, too", said the Captain, "another thing happened called 'The American Civil Rights Movement'. You may have noticed that I am a black man."

Ant shrugged.

"He's always been observant", said Cleo acidly.

"Well, back in the nineteen sixties, a man like me would have been unable to ride the same bus as a white man in some southern states of the USA; and around that time a lot of black men and women joined together to say a big No to all of that. A lot of changes were happening, and a lot of military and government people didn't like it. And those military and government people who were in charge of America's secret colonies in space thought it would be just dandy if they could keep those colonies just the apple-pie way America *used* to be, with no uppity blacks, no hippies, and no gook-loving liberals."

"That's terrible", said Ant. "Except about the hippies, of course."

"*Ant!*" hissed Cleo. "This is *serious!*"

"Word started to get about", said the Commodore. "Lists of troublemakers were being drawn up. Arrests were being planned."

"And it's at about this time", said the Captain, "that we stop talking about 'the troublemakers' and start talking about 'us'."

"The twelve most populous American colonies were the first ones to revolt", said the Commodore. "Then the British colony at Lalande was ordered to give support to US vessels fighting the rebellion - effectively, to fire on the same crews who'd been their NATO allies only the day before. They refused, declared their world independent, and threw their lot in with the rebels."

"America counterattacked, of course", said the Captain. "Their oldest and biggest colony at Alpha Centauri, which you may know better as Newer England, was recaptured within days. The rebel worlds had no means of fighting back at first. But soon they learned strength in numbers. Under Doctor Levi Morgan, they formed the United States of the Zodiac on St. Jude's Day, 1974, and elected Dr. Morgan their first President. Since that day, the USA hasn't dared attack further."

"Why not?" said Ant.

The Captain chuckled. "Dr. Morgan threatened to land a saucer on the White House lawn and tell the truth about America's colonies in space to every journalist in DC. It was the only card he had to play. But it worked. The generals were terrified. The USZ has been left to its own devices for the last twenty-five years."

"What happened to the American rebels on Alpha Centauri?" said Cleo.

"We don't know for certain", said the Commodore uneasily. "But intelligence sources tell us that one of Alpha Four's largest continents now has several large, regular structures in its central desert - structures that could house up to ten thousand people. It's in about this area that early surveys of Alpha Four indicated deposits of uranium oxide so rich that they could probably be mined by a man with a shovel. Certain evidence - incoming shovel quotas, outgoing uraninite shipments - suggest to us that the prisoners on Alpha Four are doing just that."

Glenn Bob's jaw dropped. "Pitchblende? Being mined by *hand,* by *men?*"

"And women", said the Commodore. "And children."

"But - but - they'd *die*", said Glenn Bob.

"Intelligence reports indicate that the amount of activity on the site has been decreasing in recent years, yes", said the Captain drily.

"And Lalande 21185?" said Cleo.

"American forces helped the British recapture it", said the Commodore. "They met with little resistance. However, by that time the Lalande 2 colony had been independent for nearly a year, and during that year, a British long range exploration vessel had come limping back in to Lalande 2. The Lalandese had given up all hope of seeing the crew of that ship alive again. I was particularly happy to see at least one of them, as he was my father. He told us a story of a habitable planet in a location nobody would ever find us, or even think of looking. The reason why the British and Americans met little resistance when they recaptured Lalande 2 was that the Lalandese had already left the planet and come here, to Gondolin. And hence those Lalandese became Gondoliers."

Then, the Commodore turned his attention to Glenn Bob, who had the uneasy expression of someone trying to find a way not to believe what he was being told.

"We'll find your family, Captain", he said. "If they can be found."

"The *United States AeroSpace Navy* will find them", said Glenn Bob.

"The USASN", said Captain Yancy, "has been lied to. It will not even begin looking for your family. It's been told the Soviets killed them, and that's the sort of lie the USASN likes to believe. The Soviets, meanwhile, have been told the Zodiac Navy killed them, and *they* probably believe *that.* The only people likely to look for your folks, right now, are looking at you, right now."

Glenn Bob stared at the floor sourly, but said nothing. Captain Yancy walked over to him, clapped his arms on Glenn Bob's shoulders, and said:

"I know you don't believe me, son. You believe the US Zee are a bunch of pinko Commie nigger hippy good for nothings, don't you. You probably feel dirty just being touched by a big old piccaninny like me. But I'm going to do a deal with you. I am going to give you the skills and the tools to be a US Zee flight officer. Only a US Zee officer, you see, is going to have any chance of finding your mom and dad, and to be frank, I need all the US Zee officers I can get. In particular, I need the sort of man who can steal an advanced fighter from under the noses of the Soviet military. After all, I'm only a piccaninny, after all, albeit one with a PhD in n-dimensional geometry."

At the words 'n-dimensional geometry', Ant was sure he saw Glenn Bob's eyes flicker; but the New Dixielander said nothing. Captain Yancy clapped Glenn Bob on the shoulders again and stood up. "Do we got that deal?"

Glenn Bob was still looking at the floor, but nodded sullenly.

Captain Yancy looked round at Ant and Cleo. "Since we're talking about the attack on Croatoan", he said, "I'm confused. If you claim neither the Soviets nor the USZ carried out the attack, then who did?"

"Someone whose ship looks like God's clean air on radar, and a big old Cuban cigar to the naked eye", said Ant. He looked at Glenn Bob. Glenn Bob looked back at him and nodded slowly in agreement. "And someone who leaves a weird blue paste behind that flows over any living stuff it touches."

The Commodore exchanged glances with the Captain. The glances were not encouraging.

"What?" said Ant. "What have I said?"

There was an uncomfortable silence.

"There's, ah, only ever been one recorded instance of ships that don't show up on any form of radar", said the Captain slowly. "Certainly in combination with any evidence of a substance of the sort that you describe."

"Well", said Cleo, folding her arms and settling into a chair, "we're waiting."

"In 1947", said the Captain, "a flight of USAAF P-80 jet fighters encountered an unidentified aircraft which they then engaged and, uh, neutralized."

"Yes, we heard all this in Croatoan", said Ant. "They were attacked by it and shot it down."

The Captain shifted from foot to foot uncertainly.

"Are you saying they *weren't* attacked by it?" said Cleo.

"That is", said the Captain, "the official story."

"And the unofficial story is?"

"I can only suppose", said Captain Yancy uncomfortably, "that it behaved in some manner that they imagined to be threatening."

"But it didn't fire on them."

"I am ashamed to report", said the Captain, "that it didn't. There's little wonder the USAAF pilots were spooked, mind you. They almost flew straight into it. Reported that they saw no trace on their radar screens throughout. Examination of the ground wreckage revealed, among other things, a curious organic paste of exactly the same type that you described, which seemed to possess a curious affinity with living tissue. One of the examining technicians was killed by the material, and it was decided after some deliberation to destroy it."

"Wise decision", shuddered Ant.

"You're absolutely sure this...paste was present", said the Commodore.

"It was present *all over Ant*", said Cleo.

"Ah", said the Commodore. He and the Captain exchanged another meaningful glance.

"Quit exchanging meaningful glances there", said Glenn Bob, "and tell us what you're thinking."

"Well", said the Captain, "several weeks ago, a USZ deep space frigate, *Xenophon,* was discovered drifting in unpatrolled space, completely undamaged, but *completely deserted*. Meals were half eaten on the tables in her galley. A computer game was still playing on a monitor. And the same sticky residue was everywhere, on all surfaces. Luckily, this time the boarding party were wearing space suits."

"And you think that whatever attacked Croatoan, attacked that ship as well."

"Either that", said the Commodore, "or we are the victims of a particularly vicious hoax. I'm not sure which."

"Why a hoax?" said Cleo.

"Because someone might have a lot to gain by ensuring the USA and USZ, or the USA and the Soviets, declare open war on one another", said Ant grimly.

"Very perceptive", said the Captain. "Everyone in space, you see, knows the Roswell story, and for this reason, everyone in space has been searching for the Saucerers, the intelligent aliens who must have built that vessel, for the last fifty years. And they've found nothing. Not so much as a discarded alien mind probe. We've found *life* in abundance on over thirty Earthlike worlds. But nothing intelligent. Many of our scientists have begun to openly doubt the Saucerers ever existed. But the Saucerers are still ideal raw material for any hoaxer looking to conceal his identity."

"But why would anyone pretend to be an alien to start a war?" said Ant. "Surely he'd pretend to be a Zodiacker or an American or a Russian."

Captain Yancy nodded shrewdly, as if he hadn't actually considered this.

"There is, of course", said Cleo, "another possibility."

The Captain and Commodore nodded.

"The Saucerers exist. You shot down their ship back in 1947, without provocation. And now they've come back looking for it."

The Commodore cleared his throat. "Ahem, yes, that is a *possibility*, as you say, but of course, hardly *likely*." He slid back the top of his cane, which seemed to have a number of small, home-made buttons inside it. Ant was intrigued by the fact that the button he pressed was labelled SUMMON BATMAN.

After a few seconds' wait, a man in USZ uniform marched in. He moved like a castle on a chessboard, seeming to be unable to walk diagonally. He stamped up to the Commodore and saluted him extravagantly.

"Splendid", said the Commodore. "This is Mr. McNaught, my batman."

"Your *what*?" Ant could not keep a straight face.

The Commodore was puzzled. "My batman. Is there anything odd about that?"

Ant scratched his head. "Well, sir, it's just that, on *our* planet, a Batman is a crime-fighting gentleman with a big rubber chest."

"I see. How extraordinary. Well, on *this* planet, a batman is a senior officer's assistant." He peered at Mr. McNaught accusingly. "*Do* you fight crime, Mr. McNaught?"

Mr. McNaught stood to attention with painful smartness. "EVERY CHANCE I GETS - *SAH*!"

"Jolly good. Be a brick and take these ladies and gentlemen and their, ah, mollusc to the OC's Nursery, will you, please?"

Mr. McNaught stiffened. "Are you *sure*, sir?"

"Oh yes, quite sure, quite sure. Nobody using it, after all. Carry on."

Mr. McNaught saluted, turned on his heel and stamped out of the room. When he reached the doorway and realised no-one was following him, he relaxed, slouched back into the room like a civilian, and said, "Well, come on, then."

"Do we have to do the hand-swingy-marchy-saluty thing?" said Ant.

"Not if you don't want to", said the Commodore.

Ant tapped his forehead with his fingertips and scurried from the room. Glenn Bob did a full military salute, and Cleo curtsied. Even Truman J. Slughound waved his eyestalks gently. All three of them followed Ant and Mr. McNaught.

***

The Commodore's batman showed them into a room the size of a rich man's wardrobe. Despite the fact that it had obviously been cut out of solid stone, though, the floor was even and the walls were smooth. They also had pictures of mermaids and sea horses on them.

"Mind the roof", said Mr. McNaught. "The CO used to 'ave a special pair of walkin' legs for coming in here. Looks like Mrs. Drummond's put you some grub out an' made your beds up, an' I 'opes you're grateful."

Cleo regarded the grub critically.

"It's blue", she said.

Mr. McNaught shrugged. "*Instaraquae* is this week's experimental lichen of choice", he said. "Accordin' to Catering & Nutrition, it contains nothin' that will actually kill you. Well, kill 'amsters, anyway. They always tests it on 'amsters."

Cleo stared at the food. "Has this food been tested on *animals?*"

"Certainly 'ope so, Miss." Mr. McNaught swung his head back out under the doorway. "I'm 'avin' some meself in 'alf an hour. You can always not eat any food if you wish." He looked round at the walls. "Never seen a sea 'orse meself", he said. "Can they be ridden?"

"Of course", said Cleo haughtily, as if Mr. McNaught were very very stupid. "Or else what would mermaids ride to play water polo?"

Mr. McNaught absorbed this information sagely. "A great honour, the old man allowin' you into these quarters, mind", he said. "'E's kept 'em more or less the same since the Accident."

Cleo looked at the triple-decker bunk bed warily. "Would that be the sort of Accident that takes away more than just one child?"

McNaught nodded. "Very perceptive, miss. The CO 'ad three little girls. Would've been your age by now. They used to sneak on board diplomatic ships, get a free ride out to other worlds - King, Laputa, Elysium. One day they snuck on to one ship too many. That ship never come back, an' because their names never got entered on the passenger roster, we didn't even know they was on it for five days. The ship was in good condition, the pilot was an old 'and, no navigation 'azards was reported along their course. Not a speck of wreckage was ever found. Fair broke their mother's heart."

Cleo stared glumly at the sea horses, flowers and fairies dancing round the walls.

McNaught cleared his throat. "The shower roster's been cleared for all three of you, by the way, ladies and gents, on account of your dire state of need."

"*DIRE STATE OF NEED*?"

Glenn Bob and Ant sniffed their armpits, hugely offended.

"Yes, young sirs and madam, I'm afraid it *is* that bad."

"*AND MADAM*?"

"And madam, ma'am." McNaught pointed to a locker by the three-man bunk bed. "You're honoured. Central Stores've allocated you one 'ole cake of soap." He stared at the soap hungrily, as if this was the most outlandish luxury. "Oh, an' memsahib Drummond also thought to provide for your, erm, animal." He nodded at the locker on the other side of the bunk. A battered Mr. Potato Head doll was lying on the locker in a plastic bowl into which someone had taken the trouble to burn the letters TRUMAN J. SLUGHOUND.

"I hope it's not polyethylene", said Glenn Bob. "Polyethylene gives him the guts." He looked up at McNaught. "You do realise he'll eat the bowl as well, sir."

McNaught nodded. "That thought 'ad occurred to me, but does not seem to 'ave occurred to Mrs. Drummond."

Glenn Bob grinned. "I'll hide the bowl in the locker. Tell the lady thanks."

McNaught smiled and left.

19 - Wakey Wakey Rise And Shine

Ant opened his eyes. It was still Not All A Dream.

His feet were sticking out of the end of the bed. The bed had, after all, been made for an eight-year-old girl. But despite this, Ant was going to stay in it for *ever*.

A horrible image loomed into view. Ant focussed on it. It was the bright and breezy face of Commodore Drummond, who was *already* wearing a uniform.

"Good morning, young astronaut! Up and dressed, chop chop! We have to be off to the sickbay!"

"But I'm not sick", mumbled Ant, as Mr. McNaught pulled him up and out of bed and manoeuvred him into a dressing gown.

"No, but those we know and love are", said the Commodore, "and we must visit them." Behind Ant, Mr. McNaught lifted Cleo, still fast asleep, clean out of bed, and deposited her into a pair of fluffy slippers. The slippers had mermaids and seahorses on them. Ant noticed the Commodore wiping a tear from his eye.

"Wha?" said Cleo in confusion. "I'm not in bed any more."

"Observant child", said the Commodore proudly. Ant noticed that Truman J. Slughound was gliding menacingly around Commodore Drummond's ankles like a circling shark.

"Uh, sir", he said, pointing at the officer's boots.

The Commodore glanced down. "What? Ah, of course." He pulled a trouser leg up to reveal a length of gleaming steel. "All metal legs today, you see. I fear nothing!"

"Poor old Truman J.", said Cleo blearily, brushing her teeth using a brush produced by Mr. McNaught, "he probably thinks your ankles are still edible."

"I think", confided the Commodore, "that he might be after the tiddlywinks in my pocket." He pulled a hand out of his trousers, revealing a bright green plastic disc held between his fingers. The sluggie pricked up his eyes in excitement, and he stopped his circling and followed the tiddlywink like a dog watching a biscuit. "Aha, now he is in my power", gloated the Commodore. He tiddled the wink into the air, and the sluggie reared up and gobbled it down with a noise like a giant squid gargling with Space Dust.

Mr. McNaught handed Cleo a little girl's dress, hand-stitched with flowers, seahorses, and mermaids, and hung a uniform shirt and trousers over the end of Glenn Bob's bed. Glenn Bob was still snoring soundly. Cleo held the pretty frock at arm's length, rather as if it had been a dead rat; then, she put it down carefully, picked up Glenn Bob's uniform, and went off to the showers to dress.

"Extraordinary", said the Commodore. "I see I have a good deal to learn about the changing face of pre-teen fashion. Mr. McNaught, another uniform if you will."

"Rats", complained Ant. "Can't Glenn Bob wear the dress?"

"He doesn't have the legs for it", said the Commodore. "And come to think of it, neither do I."

Soon, Ant, Cleo and Glenn Bob were all dressed.

"You two look like boy scouts", accused Cleo.

"*You,*" said Ant, "look like someone who gets all her clothes from Army Surplus."

"Just because yours don't fit", said Cleo smugly, and twirled for everyone's benefit.

"No time for a fashion show", said the Commodore. "Off to the sickbay. Quick time!"

"Who are we going to see?" said Cleo, struggling to keep up with the Commodore as he stalked out of the bedroom down a rough-cut, dimly-lit passageway spiralling downward. "Ow!" she added. Her head had hit the roof, which was so low that Ant and Glenn Bob also had to stoop. Mr. McNaught was almost bent double. The Commodore, Ant noticed, did not appear to be suffering from the low ceiling height.

"Pardon me, sir, but your legs seem shorter today", said Ant.

"Thought I'd go for a short walk today", winked the Commodore. "Aha, here we are."

The sickbay was rather larger than in Croatoan, and also looked fuller. Maybe, thought Ant, people injured themselves more often on Gondolin. There was a man opposite Ant whose face had broken out in purple blotches, and another next to him whose arm seemed to have swelled up like a balloon.

"Nettle sting", grimaced the Commodore. "He took two spines in the arm."

Both men saluted, the Commodore, the balloon-armed man with some difficulty, though cheerily enough. The Commodore saluted back.

"Fine pair of chaps", he whispered. "I don't know a better pair of chaps. Nice to see them looking well, what?"

"What's wrong with the purple man?" said Cleo.

"Gondolier's Mug", said the Commodore, waving his hand airily as if having gigantic purple blotches breaking out on your cheeks was nothing. "A harmless form of lichen that grows on your face. Everyone here gets it sooner or later."

Cleo pursed her lips in a way that suggested she did not consider anything that grew on her face to be harmless, but said nothing.

"And here", said the Commodore, "is our patient."

The man in the final bed was a patchwork of dressings. Despite this, he was sitting happily playing with a plastic toy UFO which had INFINITE SPACE INVADER OBJECT MADE IN JAPAN printed down one side of it. He was making happy exploding and whooshing noises.

"Richard", said the Commodore. "I see you are making a splendid recovery."

Mr. Turpin looked up at the Commodore sharply. Almost in the blink of an eye, he seemed to weaken and wilt until he scarcely seemed able to hold his flying saucer.

"Oh gosh, sir", he said, "I do feel so terribly ill."

"Nonsense, you look perfectly able to return to active duty. You may be interested to know that Penelope Farthing has taken your Fantasm out for a spin."

Turpin looked confused. "I've got a *Fantasm*?"

"You really don't remember", said Ant. "Do you."

Mr. Turpin squinted at Ant. Ant noticed some of his fingertips were still bandaged. "I remember you", said Mr. Turpin. Cleo glowered at him. "Ah, um. Yes, I remember *both* of you."

"And you are *very, very* sorry", said Commodore, arms folded, staring down at Turpin with a seriousness Ant had not seen in him before. "Aren't you."

The Highwayman hung his head. "Um. Yes, I am."

"You took this young lady and gentleman light years from their homes and families and put their lives in danger. On top of that, I have had to Indoctrinate them."

Ant blinked in alarm. "I don't remember being indoctrinated", he said.

"Um, 'indoctrinated' just means that you've been told flying saucers and colonies in space and Gondolin exist", explained Mr. Turpin. "It's quite a serious matter, actually. If you get indoctrinated and then don't agree to breathe a word of what you've heard when you get back to Earth, then we have to -"

"And on top of that", interrupted the Commodore, "you lost your entire consignment of unnaturally flavoured monosodium glutamate crisps. Memsahib Drummond is most *dreadfully* upset. We had heard that Walker's were bringing out a Mango Chutney flavour."

"I'm dreadfully sorry, sir", squirmed Turpin.

"But you *did* bring back a Fantasm", beamed the Commodore. "Though through no fault of your own, it would appear." His beam disappeared. He pointed to Glenn Bob. "*This* young gentleman aided your escape from the Americans."

Mr. Turpin looked at Commodore Drummond blankly. "Americans, sir? It, er, wasn't Americans. It was the Special Operations first of all, then, er -" his face went blank a moment, "Russians later on. For some reason."

"Special Operations were the men we saw in the wood", said Ant. "Weren't they."

"Yes", said Ant. "Yes, that's right. A top secret tentacle of the UK government. They'd pulled in one of our Irregulars, Quantrill, sir, and they must have gotten the place and time we were loading up the Astromoke out of him. Luckily for me, Drague still always turns up to a bust in that great big car of his. As soon as I saw it through the trees, I knew what was going on and ran, though one of them took a shot at me and wounded me in the hand."

The Commodore frowned. "George Quantrill. A good man. A pity."

"George volunteered to infiltrate Earth society for us and buy up goods we needed", explained Mr. Turpin to Ant, Glenn Bob and Cleo. "That's what an Irregular is."

"But you can build flying saucers", said Ant. "You're miles ahead of anyone on Earth. What do you need to buy stuff on Earth for?"

The Commodore shifted from prosthesis to prosthesis in embarrassment. "Out here, there are many products we simply cannot, erm, produce", he admitted. "No matter what replacement compounds we may synthesize, for example, there are still many purposes for which natural rubber is still superior. And there are also many complex electronic and mechanical devices which we just don't have the capacity to build, but which we nevertheless still desperately require."

"And you still like your malt whisky", said Ant.

The Commodore looked at the floor guiltily, but said nothing.

"And your prawn cocktail crisps", said Cleo.

The Commodore cleared his throat nervously. "I can see you understand us perhaps a little better than we would like. What happens, as you've guessed, is that we send out the occasional ship, under the command of one of our very best pilots, to run the gauntlet of the Earth's defences and land a very brave man on Earth who then tries to acquire some of these items, these devices, these substances, these *crisps*, that we cannot manufacture here. George Quantrill was one such man. He was acting in the very best interests of his town and colony. I assure you there were items in that cargo that were sorely needed for our colony's survival. George Quantrill was not lost for crisps alone."

"Mr. Quantrill's cover wasn't good enough", said Cleo.

"No", agreed Turpin. "He was rumbled when he checked into a hospital after getting stung by a nettle. Earth people don't do that", he said, "erm, apparently."

"What'll happen to Mr. Quantrill now?" said Ant.

"If he's lucky", said the Commodore darkly, "they'll kill him."

"They can't do that", protested Cleo. "He has rights. Since 1969, Britain has not had the Death Penalty."

"Mr. Quantrill", said Turpin through gritted teeth, "doesn't exist. He was not born on Earth, so no-one will notice if he dies on it."

"We lose many of our very best men this way", said the Commodore. "We land them outside some English town, and they try to get jobs and places to stay and beaver along just like any normal Earthman. But sooner or later, the fact that they *aren't* Earthmen always catches them out. One of our Irregulars asked the stewardess in a British Airways jet why the plane didn't just take off and land vertically. Another one only ever travelled by tube across London and held a heavy book over his head all the time he was outdoors in case it rained acid on him. Our level of knowledge of basic Earth life gets more outdated day by day. I, for example, believed until recently that young people would be seen dead in public wearing flared trousers." He laughed at his own naïveté.

"Young people *are* seen in public wearing flared trousers", said Cleo defiantly. "It's called Retro Chic."

The Commodore shrugged, smiled and spread his arms wide helplessly.

"*We* can tell you what young people would be seen in public wearing", blurted Ant.

"Pardon?" said the Commodore.

Ant felt foolish. He could feel his ears begin to redden. "Well", he started uncertainly, particularly since Cleo was glaring at him, "we *are* normal Earthmen, er, Earthboys, er, Earthgirls, Earthchildren. *We* know what Earth people do and don't do."

The Commodore's expression lit up with joy, so suddenly that Ant had a peculiar feeling he had been railroaded. "*Really*?" He slid back the top of his cane and pushed one of his makeshift buttons, which Ant was disturbed to see was labelled SUMMON DEVERIL.

Cleo nudged Ant. "Maybe the Commodore's a dyslexic satanist", she whispered.

The Commodore tapped his feet impatiently. Occasionally, he rolled up his sleeve, looked at his watch, and tutted.

"Capital fellow, Deveril", he said. "But not strong on punctuality."

Eventually, the door to the sickbay opened and a young man burst in clutching a sheaf of papers. His hairdo, Ant noted with some alarm, was not a mullet, but a peculiar Style With No Name that grew long on one side of his face and short on the other. So long was this hair that only one of his eyes was visible, giving him the appearance of a sullen teenager. He wore what seemed to be a Volkswagen car badge around his neck on a chain, and a pink T shirt which seemed, bafflingly, to stop short of his navel.

The Commodore noticed Ant staring at the young man's hairdo.

"Mr. Deveril is excused a sensible haircut on account of his Earth Familiarisation duties", he said. "He is our Earth Familiarisation Officer."

"Sorry I'm late, sir", said Deveril, saluting and dropping several of his papers. "I had a number of nearly new copies of *Vogue, Railway Modeller,* and *Soldier of Fortune* to read."

"Mr. Deveril", said the Commodore, "may I introduce two *genuine Earth people.*" He indicated Ant and Cleo proudly.

"Hmm." Mr. Deveril squinted at them critically. He walked round the back of them and looked them up and down.

"Not bad, not bad. The uniforms would give them away back in Blighty, of course. And *these* things", he said, fingering Cleo's hair extensions, "are just *so* Seventies. Does anyone on Earth still want to look like Bob Marley? I don't think so!" He opened Cleo's mouth with his fingers. She snapped at them. He jumped back and snatched his papers to his chest.

"Uh, the dental work is also *far* too good for England", he said. "I would suggest poor quality amalgam fillings in some of the molars, and maybe ripping out an incisor or two. And the boy's look is hopeless. He should really be back-combing his hair more, and adding maybe a touch of eyeliner. The New Romantics -"

"These two", repeated the Commodore heavily, still smiling though through gritted teeth, "are *genuine Earth people.*"

Mr. Deveril stopped dead cold short in his tracks.

He stared from Ant to Cleo, and from Cleo to Ant.

"No", he said, in wonder.

"But yes", said the Commodore. "I thought it might be appropriate for them to spend an hour or two with you in order to discuss current Earth trends and fashions."

"Oh yes", said Mr. Deveril, gazing at Ant in awe, "most certainly, yes! Genuine Earth people, here!" He grabbed Ant's hand and pumped it up and down. "It's an honour, believe me. An honour!" He stepped a little closer to Cleo. "Tell me - how is the Quo's latest album?"

"What", said Cleo in annoyance, "is the Quo?"

Mr. Deveril stared at Cleo aghast, as if she'd told him England had sunk beneath the waves and was no longer commonly believed in by anyone but Charles Berlitz.

"The Quo", he repeated. "The Quo - is the *Quo*."

"I can see you have a great deal to talk about", said the Commodore.

20 - Elvis Is Dead

"Freddie Mercury is *dead*?"

"I'm afraid so", said Cleo solemnly. "He has gone to the great jamming session in the sky, along with Kurt Cobain and John Lennon."

"John Lennon is *dead*? And who is Kurt Cobain?"

Mr. Deveril's office was tinier even than the Commodore's nursery, and was wallpapered with tat. Faded, dog-eared copies of *Empire, TV Times, Variety* and *The Face* hung from the roof on string, and the walls themselves were plastered with bits of junk mail and excess packaging which any normal household would have thrown away, but which here were treasured, stuck in pride of place, carefully manoeuvred into position so that no edges overlapped. Cinema tickets, Student Union cards, theatre posters all jostled for space on the curved walls. Plastic McDonald's figurines and lava lamps jostled for space on the shelves.

"Marc Bolan's dead too", said Ant sarcastically.

"I know Marc Bolan's dead!" said Mr. Deveril. "You know, I could be forgiven for thinking you people think I'm some sort of fool."

"And Elvis", said Cleo, "Elvis is dead."

"He is not", said Ant. "My Dad says he's been seen in Las Vegas." Cleo and Ant locked hard stares for several seconds. Then Ant turned to Mr. Deveril again. "The hair, by the way", he said, "must go." This time Cleo nodded firmly.

Deveril touched his hair protectively. "Why? What do men wear their hair like on Earth today?"

Ant thought a moment. "Well...sort of like, everyone looking normal, like everyone else."

Deveril shuddered. "It sounds terrible", he said.

"You should also lose the VW medallion", said Ant.

Deveril fingered the car badge in desperation, as if his mother planet was turning against him. "Do people not *wear* these any more?"

"Cars yes", said Ant. "People no. Though if it was gold plated", he thought suddenly, "you could pass for a drug dealer."

"I *would* say", said Cleo, looking at Deveril's bare midriff, "that the T shirt must go too. But it seems to be halfway on the way out already."

Deveril stared at the shirt. "But this is straight out of *Dallas*!" he wailed.

"Hmm", said Cleo. "I think I see the problem here". She picked up a dog-eared copy of *Vogue* on Mr. Deveril's desk and flipped it open to a page where a stick-thin model was sauntering down a catwalk dressed as a velour shark, complete with teeth, fins and tail.

"What you have to realise", she said, "is that people on Earth don't actually dress like this."

Mr. Deveril stared at the magazine uncomprehendingly. "You mean you just *pretend*?"

Cleo thought about this for a moment. "Yes", she said. "Yes, that's fair. Women all spend hundreds of pounds a year on fashion magazines that tell them everyone dresses like this, and then they go out and buy another nice white top and another pair of Levis."

Mr. Deveril was appalled. "Why?" he said.

Cleo shrugged and made a face that said *You tell me*.

"Men do something very similar", said Ant. "But without the 'spend hundreds of pounds on magazines' part."

"Blue jeans, a white cotton shirt, a cheap pair of trainers and a crew cut will make any man fade into the background on any street in England", said Cleo. "As will", she added, "a suit and tie."

"But I thought the hippies had cast off the square oppressive clothing of the Man!" said Deveril desperately.

"I think the hippies thought so too", said Cleo. "Most of them wear suits these days. And work with computers."

"Then the Man won", said Deveril.

"Yup", said Cleo. "Man one, hippies, nil."

Deveril grimaced. "Earth sounds like a terrible place to live."

"Oh, it is", sighed Cleo. "Some days you can't get a decent latte two days straight."

Deveril thought about this. "Wait a minute. If it's such a terrible place to live, why are you so interested in going *back* there?"

"Because it's a terrible place to live where I can get a hot bath any time I like, I can eat food in colours other than turquoise and purple, and women's underwear comes in varieties other than blue Airtex", said Cleo, smiling sweetly.

"Oh", said Mr. Deveril; and then, seizing a pen, with absolute sincerity, added:

"Can you describe any of this women's underwear to me?"

***

"ANT! CLEO! I've been doing me some NON-EUCLIDEAN GEOMETRY!"

Glenn Bob's face was the same as Lieutenant Farthing's had been when Commodore Drummond had told her there was a Soviet fighter in her garage.

"Oh", said Ant. "Uh, I suppose that'll be Geometry that's Non-Euclidean, then."

"Doctor Allison says I do mathematics real well", said Glenn Bob. "She says I might make Navigator or Pilot."

Ant thought about this. "I'd rather be a pilot", he said.

"I'd rather be a Navigator", said Glenn Bob. "There's more mathematics involved."

The thought that anyone might deliberately do mathematics for some twisted form of pleasure was difficult for Ant to take in easily. He stared hard at Glenn Bob for some sign that the other boy was not entirely serious. There was no such sign. Glenn Bob had only been on Gondolin a day, and already looked as if he belonged in his uniform. Ant, meanwhile, felt more alien with every passing hour.

Glenn Bob was sitting next to a severe-looking woman with grey hair and steel-rimmed spectacles.

"Excuse me, ma'am", said Ant, "but are you Doctor Allison? We were told to report here to you. The Commodore said you'd saved us seats."

The lady nodded stiffly and pointed at two empty spaces next to herself. Ant and Cleo crowded into them gratefully.

The room around Ant was familiar. The same pictures and posters lined the curving walls. The same lady in the Marks and Spencer's dress scowled down from the photograph.

"*You'd think she'd have more fashion sense in space in 1999*", whispered Ant. "*She should have giant plastic boots and big pointy shoulders or something. She looks like she bought that in our High Street.*"

"*Ant*", whispered Cleo in embarrassment, "*that's the* Queen."

"*Oh*", said Ant.

"*And that man she's shaking hands with is the Commodore. It must be a VERY old photo.*"

"*Crikey, yes*", whispered Ant. "*He has legs in it.*"

"WELCOME, ANTHONY STEVENS AND CLEOPATRA SHAKESPEARE", bellowed the Commodore from the front of the crowd, "TO OUR TOWN HALL."

The room was different from the last time that Ant and Cleo had been in it, because it was now full of people. The tables had been folded back or cleared away, and twenty or thirty Gondoliers with assorted military and peculiar hairstyles were sitting in rows up and down the room, chattering excitedly. When the Commodore announced Ant and Cleo, however, the chattering stopped. A sea of eyes turned towards them, gawping at them whilst trying to appear to be gawping at something slightly to the side of them.

The chattering became whispering.

"*Isn't it* amazing*! They look* exactly like us*!*"

"*Apart from the strange hairstyles.*"

"*They're called* dreadlocks*, I believe. All Earth women wear them now. Even the Queen.*"

The Commodore was already making his way toward them through the crowd. At one point he stopped, grabbed hold of a blonde woman supporting the most mountainous back-combed beehive Ant had ever seen, and dragged her by the elbow towards Ant and Cleo, saying such things as "*You* really *must meet them. They will be so delighted.*"

Once the woman saw them, she adopted a massive insincere smile, like a shark wearing lipstick.

"May I introduce our resident *fashionista*, Miss Michelle Enlyfrith", said the Commodore.

Michelle Enlyfrith extended enormous pink fingernails like a velociraptor's. "You must be the young lady from Earth everyone's talking about. I can't *wait* to discuss the latest modes with you."

"I can see", said Cleo drily, looking Miss Enlyfrith up and down, "that we're going to have quite a long discussion."

Miss Enlyfrith went whiter than her foundation, and titters travelled through the crowd like wind through grass. Appearing to notice nothing, the Commodore released her and strode forward to the front of the crowd, leaning heavily on his stick. Eventually, he reached a dais where a small high desk and chair had been set up. Opening the desk top, he took out a black tricorn hat and dull metal chain, which he hung over himself as he settled into the chair, and a gavel, with which he gently thwacked the desk lid.

"As elected mayor, I call this meeting of the Gondolin Town Council to order. Items tabled for discussion include the possibility of making workable underpants out of wood fibre, the current soft toilet paper shortage, and the proposed repatriation of three foreign nationals, Mr. Anthony Stevens and Miss Cleopatra Shakespeare of the United Kingdom of Great Britain and Ireland, and Mr. Glenn Bob Linklater of the United States of America. I propose to skip to this final point since", his eyes travelled beadily around the chamber, "that appears to be what most people have attended this meeting for."

"Speak for yourself, your worship", said a gruff voice from the crowd. "I for one care deeply for soft toilet paper." Laughter rustled through the audience.

Ant fidgeted nervously. Now he was here, he wasn't entirely sure he *wanted* to be returned to cold wet England in the first form secondary. Unfortunately, however, Cleo's hand had already shot up. It was like being at school all over again.

"The Council recognises Miss Shakespeare", said the Commodore.

"If it please your worship", said Cleo, "It is imperative I return to Earth as soon as possible. I have a grade three violin examination *and* mock Eleven Plusses to attend to. I have been spirited away from my home planet against my will."

The Commodore coughed. "Yes. I am really quite sorry about that, you know. All I can say is that Richard Turpin is one of our very finest officers, and I'm sure he had the very best of reasons for his actions."

There was a general murmur of assent from the crowd, and much nodding.

"Mr. Turpin", said Cleo firmly, "abducted us from our parents and our families. And we would very much like to go back to them, please."

"Ah, but", said the Commodore, pointing at Cleo with his gavel, "It's not quite as simple as all that, you see. If we send you back to Earth, and you start blabbing like a big blabbermouth about flying saucers - if the general public on Earth finds out that we exist - our only sure weapon against the colonial powers on Earth vanishes. The British and American governments would then have nothing to lose by attacking us. And would you want an interstellar war on your conscience, young lady?"

Cleo looked as if she was about to cry. "But I want to go *HOME!*" she wailed, and stamped her foot.

"*Poor dear*", said a lady in the crowd.

"*The CO's just a big old bully*", said another.

"Please don't misinterpret what I've said", said the Commodore hastily. "We have every intention of sending you home. But you have to understand the terrible damage you can cause if we do. You can't just zip back to England, step into school and say you're sorry you're a few weeks late for roll call because you were taken up by a UFO."

"That one doesn't work", said Ant ruefully. "Trust me." The crowd giggled.

But Cleo was having none of this. "We've been missing for over a *month*, mister! What do you expect me to tell them? 'Oh mercy me, I fell over and lost my memory'?"

"Why not?" said the Commodore, and looked at Captain Yancy in puzzlement. The Captain boggled his eyeballs, shook his head, and shrugged back. *Kids nowadays.*

"We're going to need a better explanation", said Cleo, crossing her arms defiantly.

"The police on Earth are a bit hot on explanations", agreed Ant.

"We could have been kidnapped", said Cleo. "The police love to hear about children being kidnapped."

"Do they?" said the Commodore. "How odd."

"We could have been abducted by someone unprincipled, *totally* immoral", said Cleo with a delicious shiver of terror. "A man with absolutely no concept of the difference between good and evil."

"Rather than Lieutenant Turpin, you mean", clarified the Commodore. The crowd, who were evidently of the opinion that Turpin was some sort of Olympic-gold-medal-winning saint on roller skates, nodded and murmured again.

"We could have escaped from him", continued Cleo. "I could have squirmed free of my bonds and leapt heroically from a moving car."

"You'd be bound, then", said the Captain.

"A despicable fiend like that would be bound to tie me up", assured Cleo.

"You'd have to be able to lie about this", said the Captain. "Convincingly."

"Oh, I can lie", said Cleo. "I can make up all sorts of stories."

"That's as may be", said the Captain. "But what you're going to have to do is tell *exactly the same story as Mr. Stevens here.*" He nodded at Ant. "And remember every lie in that story, and be able to re-tell it, over and over again. For the rest of your life. Do you think you can do that?"

Cleo suddenly looked far less certain.

21 - Attack Of The White Van Man

"OOGAH!"

The tarmac hit Ant like a black oily hammer. Despite the ropes, he managed to roll, but the gravel still grated slivers of skin from off his arm and side.

Cleo was worse off. She hadn't rolled. She was lying motionless on the white line, moaning gently.

Suddenly, she sat up on her skinned knees and yelled into the fog at the receding lights of what might look, to a casual onlooker, like a moving car.

"CURSE YOU, RICHARD TURPIN!"

The Moving Car's lights veered upward sharply, as if it were accelerating up a hill of impossible steepness, then faded into the mist. Small bolts of tame lightning still fizzled through the grass.

"CLEO!" yelled Ant. "LOOK OUT!"

He yanked Cleo off the highway just before a *real* set of car headlights steamed straight through the space where she'd been sitting ranting at Mr. Turpin. The lights were accompanied by a blare from the horn, and an enraged look from the driver of the car, a big black man with a beard birds might nest in.

"Mr. Turpin set us down as gently as he could", said Ant, "considering we had to look as if we hadn't been set down gently. We had to look as if we'd jumped out of a moving car rather than stepped out of a flying saucer."

"Mr. Turpin takes vicious pleasure in the pain and suffering of others", complained Cleo. "Unlike that nice Commodore Drummond. He's quite good-looking for a gentleman of a certain age, you know."

The car had screeched to a halt a few hundred yards further on. Ant suspected the driver of the car was about to give himself and Cleo a Bloody Good Piece Of His Mind.

"Cleo, the Commodore hasn't got any *legs*."

"He doesn't need legs in space. Though Mr. Turpin's better-looking, I think."

Ant was amazed. "You think Mr. Turpin is *good-looking*?"

"Oh, yes. He's an absolute studmuffin. *Such* a waste." Cleo began working her way backwards across the grass towards a stile leading off the road into the country park. Once she was at the stile, she pushed and wriggled herself upright.

Ant paused to think a minute.

"Wait a minute." Ant's mental processes clanked into action at lightning speed. "You *fancy* him."

"I do not. In any case, *you* fancy Lieutenant Farthing."

Ant was outraged. "Do not!"

"Do!"

The door of the car banged shut. Well-heeled shoes crunched on asphalt.

"I think", said Ant, "that it might be a good idea to not be here."

Cleo struggled up onto the top bar of the stile and wiggled her bottom towards Ant. "Well, reach around and untie my wrists, then."

Ant moved closer and worked himself upright next to her. "It might be better if we went a bit further into the woods and did it there. That big black guy looked a nasty customer."

"Just because he's black", said Cleo, "doesn't mean he's violent." Luckily, he didn't actually seem to be coming their way. Ant could see his silhouette through the fog. He was unrolling a piece of paper from a cardboard tube, and seemed to be sticking it up inside a telephone box Ant could dimly see further down the road. Maybe, Ant thought, he was a manager advertising a band.

"Hold still", said Ant. "There; I think that's done it."

"Result!" Cleo skipped away, rubbing her wrists. "Ooooh, that does feel good."

Ant waddled up onto the stile and presented his wrists. "Well, don't just stand there, numbnuts, come back here and do me."

"Never insult anyone", Cleo said, "when you've both hands tied behind your back and your back to them."

"Just because you're black", reminded Ant, "doesn't mean you're violent."

"Don't you believe it, honey boy - hang on." Cleo's voice fell quiet.

"Don't tell me", said Ant. "There's dog dirt on the top of the stile. There is, isn't there?" His face went almost wistful. "Sweet dog dirt of planet Earth, how I have missed you -"

Cleo grabbed Ant's shoulder and span him round.

The stile was plastered with Ant and Cleo's faces.

HAVE YOU SEEN THIS GIRL? shrieked a poster in huge red letters. Underneath it was a recent picture of Cleo smiling beautifully and accepting a Prize for Achievement in full school uniform. Underneath this, in handwritten letters, were the words AND THIS BOY??? and a blurry photo of Ant, looking very young, grinning weirdly with a bright red face and his hair sticking straight up in the air as if he'd been electrified.

"You look like a cretin", said Cleo.

"I was upside down on a climbing frame at the time", explained Ant. "That's funny. Mum took that picture years ago. Dad burned all of his photos when Mum left."

100 THOUSAND POUND REWARD!!!! screamed the poster; and underneath, had a third picture of a combed-haired hippy wearing a morning suit, smiling at the camera.

"Ohhh dear", said Ant. "Cleo, we have to get home straight away."

"I'm not arguing", said Cleo, "but why?"

Ant pointed at the sentence underneath the picture, which said:

HAVE YOU SEEN THIS MAN? HE IS THOUGHT TO BE INVOLVED WITH THEIR DISAPPEARANCE!

Cleo squinted at the photo. "Is that man Special Operations? I don't recognise him."

"That's my *dad*, Cleo. That's his wedding photo, minus my mum. See the tear where the photo's been ripped in half? Only my mum keeps photos like this. My mum's behind all of this, I know she is."

"I hope", said Cleo, "that your dad's not been arrested." She undid Ant's hands while he sat on the stile reading about himself.

Underneath the poster on the stile, printed on poor quality paper that had wrinkled in the rain, was a second, smaller sticker which said:

DID YOU SEE 7 OR 8 LARGE BLACK VAN'S FILLE'D WITH ARME'D MASKE'D CHILE'D ABDUCTERS ON THE M1 SOUTHBOUND BETWEEN JCTNS. 15 & 16 ON SEPTEMBER 3? IF YES, RING DAVE ON THIS NUMBER: 07714 012352.

"No", said Ant. "Purely on the basis of spelling and grammar, I think my Dad's still very much at large." He looked up the road where a telephone box marked the beginning of a village. "We could call him from here, if he'll accept the charges." He thought about this a second, then clapped Cleo on the shoulder. "Come on, let's try it anyway."

Cleo grabbed Ant by the arm. "No, Ant, I don't think so."

Ant stared at her in amazement. "Why not?"

"Look at the sticker *carefully.*"

Ant peered at it.

"Someone's put another sticker over the telephone number."

Cleo nodded. "Someone who wanted us to ring the *wrong* number. Someone who wanted *anyone* who saw any big black vans to ring the wrong number." She mouthed the words at Ant: *Special Operations.*

Ant gulped, just at the moment that a hand slammed down on the stile near Ant's own.

"GOOD MORNING", said the man on the end of the hand. He was very big. His hand looked like a pork chop someone had carved into the shape of fingers. He was cheerful enough, or at any rate, he was smiling. He was standing on the path into the country park on the other side of the stile, and was wearing a Gore-Tex parka and a pair of walking boots. He was also wearing his socks outside his trousers. Ant wondered if he knew.

"YOU LOOK A LONG WAY FROM HOME", said the man. "WOULD YOU LIKE A LIFT?"

Ant looked in the direction of the telephone box, and the village. The first house was inside spitting distance. He turned back to the man.

"How", said Ant, "do you *know* we're a long way from home?"

"OH, BUT YOU DEFINITELY LOOK A LITTLE LOST", said the man, grinning.

"Why do you have one hand behind your back?" said Cleo.

The man continued to smile broadly and climb over the stile. He was having to do this slowly, as he had one hand behind his back.

"Run", said Cleo.

Ant turned to run - and ran straight into the chest of another very large man.

"Grnk", said Ant, and collapsed onto all fours, holding his nose, which was weeping blood.

"Hey, careful with the head butts, big guy", said the man, who was holding a cardboard tube, and called out to the man on the stile, "I'm sorry, mate, I didn't see him -"

- and here the man's voice tailed off, as if he didn't quite believe what he was seeing, and he said:

"- Anthony?"

Then he looked past Ant, and said:

"...Cleo?"

Ant's vision unblurred enough for him to look up and see that the man he'd headbutted was big, black, and, if a couple of feet and a beard was taken off him, not unlike Cleo.

Cleo's dad looked past Cleo towards the man in the Gore-Tex parka. "Hey! Hey, you! I want a *word* with you! Oi!"

But the man had already turned tail, and was running towards a large, unmarked white van that had swept out of the fog behind them. The van slowed down for just long enough for him to clamber into its passenger door.

Behind Cleo's dad, another face was emerging from the mist - a greasy mop of greying hair underneath a tatty woollen hat and scarf that both said ARSENAL.

"Who's that, Len? Are you okay? I could have sworn you said - ANT! CLEO!"

Cleo forced a smile.

"Er - hi Dad", she said. "Uh, I am - *we* are - really, really *really* pleased to see you."

Glutton for punishment? Why not try these:

Ant and Cleo Volume 2: Sister Ships and Alastair

Somewhere in Bedfordshire, someone may be working on a bomb that could destroy a world. Mysterious Men in Black need Ant and Cleo to find out for sure, but they'll have to get past Flossie and the girls first...

Ant and Cleo Volume 3: There Ain't Gonna Be No World War Three

Cleo is so glad not to be going to Germany. She hates sausages, and knows for a fact that every adult German is forced to wear Lederhosen from birth. But Commodore Drummond needs Ant and Cleo in Germany - there is a thing there, long forgotten, that could change the course of the war with Earth. Unfortunately, Larry's not far behind them - and this time, he's in wolf's clothing...

Ant and Cleo Volume 4: Destination Alpha Four

In the Sunset Desert of Alpha Centauri A Four are three immense structures. For nearly thirty years, these massive mines have used United States of the Zodiac prisoners to dig uraninite out of the ground by hand. No-one escapes from Alpha Four. Once you are sent there, established wisdom considers you as good as dead.

It's time for Ant and Cleo to prove established wisdom wrong...

Ant and Cleo Volume 5: Dog On The Highway

For fifteen years, the Sternekinder have been launching pirate attacks on United States of the Zodiac shipping. If their hidden homeworld of Asgard could be found an end could be put to this, and Charity Drummond and Cleopatra Shakespeare have seen Asgard's sky - but no-one else in the cadet corps is prepared to believe Asgard even exists...

Ant and Cleo Volume 6: At The Goings Down of the Suns

Earth's problem children are coming home, and no-one's killing the fatted calf to welcome them.

Bad things are happening back in the Really Old Country. Alastair Drague is getting nervous. Things are going on in his capital city that his own people either can't or won't make head or tail of. What is going on, and is it linked to something murderously efficient out at Barnard's Star that seems to be killing United States of the Zodiac starships? Drague needs fresh minds on the problem. He needs U.S.Z. Intelligence, and its newest special agents, Anthony Stevens and Cleopatra Nefertiti Shakespeare. But Drague's own people are getting nervous about Drague himself...

Ant and Cleo Volume 7: Time Held Me Green and Dying

What is going on? Anthony Stevens is working as a hick town barnstormer; Cleopatra Shakespeare is reading fortunes in a circus; Jochen von Spitzenburg is back making coffee for his social betters in a side street café. Tamora Shakespeare and Vladlena Ilyushina are mixing with criminals, smuggling goods between Earth and Laputa. To cap it all, Elizabeth Ortega is still at large, and working with the complete assistance of Captain Yancy and Commodore Bentley Drummond. Surely this isn't the happy ending everyone worked so hard for - and whose are those spindle-shaped ships dropping out of the dull green skies of the United States of the Zodiac's capital planet?

Ant and Cleo Volume 8: The Moon a Ghostly Galleon

Someone says he knows how to work out scientifically where Asgard, the Sternekinder homeworld, might be. This comes just in time - the Sternekinder have launched attacks that have devastated five United States of the Zodiac planets, and the rest of the USZ is choked with refugees. But is the theory genius, or crackpot? And on Asgard, someone else is waiting - someone everyone had thought long dead. Someone even the Sternekinder are afraid of. But is the enemy of Ant and Cleo's enemies truly their friend?

Enjoyed this book? Help a starving fifteen stone author out and review it on Goodreads (https://www.goodreads.com/book/show/12646433-saucerers-and-gondoliers). God bless you and all who sail in you. There are also many good reasons why you shouldn't join the Dominic Green Fan Club on Facebook (https://www.facebook.com/groups/165462653826/), but you shouldn't listen to them.

9 798224 308958